"Unfinished business never goes away."

"You never really discussed your past with me all those years ago, did you?" murmured Dominic.

Katherine met his eyes steadily and said with utter truthfulness, "When I met you, I had no past and no future."

"Tell me," Dominic said, and there was a latent urgency in his voice that unsettled her.

"Tell you what?"

"Tell me what you're hiding."

She lowered her eyes. She could feel the fine prickle of perspiration. Tell him? she thought. The truth? The long, involved truth that had cost her so dear?

CATHY WILLIAMS is Trinidadian and was brought up on the twin islands of Trinidad and Tobago. She was awarded a scholarship to study in Britain, and came to Exeter University in 1975 to continue her studies into the great loves of her life: languages and literature. It was there that Cathy met her husband, Richard. Since they married, Cathy has lived in England, originally in the Thames Valley but now in the Midlands. Cathy and Richard have three daughters.

Books by Cathy Williams

HARLEQUIN PRESENTS®
2076—A NATURAL MOTHER
2105—TO TAME A PROUD HEART
2123—HIS SECRETARY BRIDE (2-in-1)

Don't miss any of our special offers. Write to us at the following address for information on our newest releases.

Harlequin Reader Service
U.S.: 3010 Walden Ave., P.O. Box 1325, Buffalo, NY 14269
Canadian: P.O. Box 609, Fort Erie, Ont. L2A 5X3

Cathy Williams

THE PRICE OF DECEIT

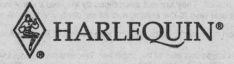

HARLEQUIN®

TORONTO • NEW YORK • LONDON
AMSTERDAM • PARIS • SYDNEY • HAMBURG
STOCKHOLM • ATHENS • TOKYO • MILAN • MADRID
PRAGUE • WARSAW • BUDAPEST • AUCKLAND

ISBN 0-373-12142-3

THE PRICE OF DECEIT

First North American Publication 2000.

Visit us at www.eHarlequin.com

Printed in U.S.A.

CHAPTER ONE

SUMMER had arrived. Katherine Lewis sat upright on the grass in Regent's Park and felt with a sort of desperate anger the tentative rays of warmth hit her skin. The least the weather could have done on this day of all days was to oblige with grey skies and rain. For the past six glorious months it had rained constantly, a never-ending drizzle that seemed to have no beginning and no end.

Everything, though, had a beginning and an end. It was the nature of things.

She shielded her eyes from the glare of the sun and, in that passing moment, she seemed to see everything; she seemed to see her entire life flash in front of her eyes, every detail of it.

Twenty years living at home with her mother in a cramped, unimaginative little terraced house in the middle of a cramped, unimaginative little terraced street in the heart of London, an existence of trying hard not to let the complaining and never-ending criticism wear her into the ground while she ploughed on with her studies and dreamed of the day when she would be free.

Well, she had at last tasted her freedom, hadn't she? It hadn't come when her mother had died, all that time ago, quietly over a cup of tea in the small unattractive sitting-room, with the television on. No, that had just been release from a sort of slavery.

Freedom had come only in the past six months.

She closed her eyes briefly and remembered, as though it was yesterday, the first time she had laid eyes on Dominic Duvall. She had stepped into that crowded room, dressed in Emma's daring clothes, with her hair in a daring style and her heart beating with terror at this new person which she had created for herself, and she had seen him standing across the room from her, tall, dark, commanding, one hand raised as he brought his glass to his lips, his other hand in his trouser pocket. Their eyes had met for a few seconds over the crowd and she had smiled and blushed and trembled in her skimpy outfit which had felt so peculiar because she had never worn anything like it in her life before.

Afterwards, he had told her that it had been the sexiest smile that he had ever seen on a woman's lips.

She lay back on the grass with her hands clasped behind her head and stared up at the sky. It was a hard blue colour. No clouds. The sort of perfect summer day which seemed designed to remind the British public at large that there was more to the weather than rain and wind.

Dominic would be here any minute.

She had decided to come ahead of him because she had a vague idea that being able to watch him approach in the distance would give her the time she needed to get herself together and do what she had to do.

She had also chosen the spot carefully, describing to him how to find her. Regent's Park, for some reason, was the one place they had not visited, and she felt that she needed to talk to him somewhere that held no memories for her.

Memories, she realised now, with a sadness that seemed to fill every pore of her body until it obliterated every other emotion, had no respect for time or place. She lay there frowning and trying to think how she would phrase what she had to say to him, and all she could think of was the way he made her feel.

Every word he had uttered to her had been a revelation, every smile a new world opening, a world which she had never even known existed.

As she walked on that tightrope which she had created for herself, he had reached out his hand, and for a while she could fly. The desperate game which had started out six months ago, a game which she knew had to be played before she lost the opportunity forever, had ended with more than she had ever bargained for.

All those people, she thought, sitting up, who said that it was better to have loved and lost than never to have loved at all, were fools.

She squinted against the sun and saw him approaching in the distance and she felt that familiar wild leap of her senses.

If someone had told her that one man could make colours seem brighter and music seem sweeter, could alter the whole tenor of her life, she would have laughed, but that was what he had done. It was as though her life had been played out in black and white and now everything was in Technicolor.

He was dressed for work. Charcoal trousers, impeccably tailored, as were all his clothes, a white shirt with the sleeves rolled to the elbows, and he was holding his jacket over one shoulder.

He was a tall man, over six feet, and with the graceful, hard build of an athlete. The sort of man who walked into a crowded room and instantly became the centre of attention. He had much more than good looks, which were no more than an accident of chance. There was something compelling about the way he carried himself, his movements unwasted and graceful, and something mesmerising about the hard lines of his face with that black hair and sea-green eyes.

In all the months they had gone out together, she had never really recovered from the wonder of knowing that he was attracted to her. *Her*!

But, she thought now, he wasn't, was he? He had never been attracted to her. He had been attracted to a vibrant, vivacious girl, a make-believe person who didn't really exist.

Katherine Lewis, she told herself with a resigned sigh, wasn't vibrant or vivacious. She was ordinary, reserved, cautious. The persona she had borrowed for the past few months, for reasons which she could never explain to him, belonged to someone else, and now she had to give it back.

She had tasted freedom, but freedom had its price and the piper had to be paid.

As he approached her he smiled, and she saw the dark charm that could entice a response from a block of ice.

'Katherine,' he said, when he was still a little way away. 'So we made it here at last.'

Out of the corner of her eye, Katherine saw the two girls who had been sunbathing a few yards away shield their eyes and covertly look at him from under their lashes. He always had that effect on the opposite sex.

'I'm sorry if I dragged you away from something important,' she said, by way of response, as he sprawled down next to her and tossed his jacket on the grass.

She didn't want to get too close to him. That would be fatal.

'Are you?' he asked lazily, turning to face her, and she tried not to succumb to the sexual warmth of his voice. 'It seems a shame to be confined to an office building when the weather is like this.'

'Fortunately,' she said, nervously keeping her distance, 'you can afford to indulge your desires to be outside, since the office building belongs to you.'

She looked at his long brown fingers and remembered the way they had touched her that first time, slowly, gently, setting her alight, so that her whole body had burned with the thrill of sensations waking for the first time.

He laughed. He had once told her that she was the most forthright person he had ever met.

'Most people seem to undergo a personality change when they're with anyone rich or powerful,' he had said. 'But you don't.'

What would he think of her if only he knew?

'Fortunately,' he agreed, slanting his eyes across to her.

'And how is it going with the project?' she asked, deciding to give herself a bit of time before she plunged into what she had to say. I love you, she told him silently in her head. I love you and I'm sorry.

'You don't really want to sit here and discuss work with me,' he drawled, lying down beside her with his arm behind his head. With a swift movement, he reached out and pulled her down beside him, laughing under his breath at her gasp, then he draped his arm over her, so that she was lying with her head on his shoulder and his hand inches away from her breast.

She felt a momentary panic and had to force herself to relax.

'I can think,' he murmured into her ear, 'of a thousand things I'd rather be doing with you than discussing work. Or at least—' he laughed, a low, amused sound that invited her to join in '—one. Why don't we go back to my apartment with a couple of bottles of champagne and some smoked salmon and let the day go by?'

'No, really, Dominic,' she muttered hurriedly, struggling to sit up.

She drew her knees up and clasped her arms around them, looking down at him. He had his eyes half closed, and his long, thick eyelashes flickered against his cheeks. There should have been something effeminate about him, but there wasn't. In fact, his face was starkly masculine.

How much you've given me, she thought; have I been selfish and cowardly? Or perhaps I have only been human.

'Yes,' he said, opening his eyes to look at her. 'Really too nice to be cooped up anywhere, even in an apartment. How about a drive?' There was a lazy glitter in his eyes that made the blood rush round her veins like a tidal flood. 'We could get in my car and just keep driving until we see somewhere we want to stop. I rather like the thought of the seaside.'

'Seasides here aren't like the ones you know,' Katherine told him, propping her chin on her knees. She knew that this aimless conversation wasn't going to get her anywhere, that she ought to say what she had to say, but now that the moment of truth had arrived she was driven by a desperate need to prolong things, to take in as much of him as she could, while she still could.

'The sea will probably be grey, the sand will be gritty and there'll be thousands of people.'

'Thank God you don't work for a travel company,' he said, and she smiled reluctantly.

'I've never been to Scotland—' you gave my life meaning, she thought. You made it all worthwhile. Have I taken too much? '—but I think the beaches up there are different. Wild and isolated.' She had never actually been anywhere. Her father had walked out on them when she was five, and from that day on her mother had counted pennies, constantly reminding her daughter that they barely had enough to buy a new pair of shoes, never mind traipse away on holidays.

'Sounds tempting.' He sat up and cupped her face in his hand. 'Let's go to Scotland.'

'Don't be foolish,' she said, reddening. His cool fingers against her skin sent a jolt of alarm through her.

'Wouldn't they give you the time off work?' he asked softly. 'I'm sure I could persuade them. Or else I could just buy the company and give you the time off.'

'No!' She had made sure not to be specific about what she was doing in London. Emma, the friend whose flat she was sharing, had fabricated that little gem to Dominic, and Katherine had consequently found herself enmeshed in a lie which she had found increasingly difficult to untell.

So many half-truths, so much shade between the light, but when you were soaring for the first time in your life it was so hard to face the crash of coming back down.

'It's nice now,' she said weakly. 'You know what the weather's like over here. By the time we made it anywhere, the sun would have changed its mind about shining and it'd be raining.'

'I'll take you to my place in the Caribbean,' he murmured. 'When it rains over there, people breathe a sigh of relief because it's good to get away from the heat.'

'Dominic Duvall, you have too much money.' Let me see you smile like that one last time, she thought, a smile that's just for me. You're the only person who did things just for me. Could you blame me for feeling special when I've never felt special in my life before?

He was looking at her, his green eyes teasing. 'Do I hear the tones of someone about to deliver a lecture?' he asked, his voice a caress, and she looked away abruptly. 'Tell me why I have too much money for my own good. No one's ever told me that before.' He trailed his finger along her arm and she shivered. 'Least of all a woman.'

'You don't know what hardship is,' Katherine said, ignoring her response to his feathery touch. 'It's like living in a bubble.'

'That makes me sound irresponsible,' he answered, smiling, 'but don't forget that my companies are responsible for the livelihoods of thousands of people.'

'I suppose so,' she said, and he sat up.

'And, believe it or not, I do care about them.'

'You don't have to justify your lifestyle to me.'

'Oh, but I do.' He stared at her so intently that her head began to swim. 'Not to anyone else—but you, yes.'

She laughed uneasily, looking away. 'It's too hot to be discussing this.'

'It's something that has to be discussed. Would you find the sort of life I lead unbearable?'

'What are you saying to me?'

He didn't answer. He fished into his jacket pocket and then held out a little box to her, and Katherine stared at it, dumbfounded and horrified.

'Go on. Take it,' he said roughly.

She still had her arms around her knees, and her fingers were digging into her skin. How could she take that box? She had known, of course, that their relationship was becoming deeper—it was one of the reasons that she had known that the time had come to break it off—but this she hadn't foreseen. She knew what was in that box. An unexploded bomb was in that box.

She reached out for it and found that her hand was shaking. Perhaps it's just a chain, she thought wildly, or a brooch, or something else harmless.

He was looking at her, and she knew that he must be misreading her nerves as excitement.

'I'm thirty-four years old,' he said in a husky voice, 'and I've never come close to doing this. Except now.'

She still hadn't opened the thing. She dropped her knees to sit cross-legged opposite him, and looked down at it in her hands. A warm breeze lifted her brown hair and blew it gently across her face. Forgive me, she thought, one day. She brushed her hair away from her face.

Before, it seemed like a thousand years ago, in another life, she had always worn her hair tied back, pulled away from her face and coiled into the nape of her neck. When she had flown to London, running as fast as her legs would take her, away from the little Midlands town where she had lived and taught, ever since her mother had died, in a little cottage that seemed to satisfy everything and nothing, away from the catastrophe that had shattered her placid existence, the first thing she had done was to unpin her hair. She had been looking for something, an adventure, and adventures did not happen to women who tied their hair at the back of their necks.

'I've known a lot of women, Katherine,' he said gravely, 'and they've all been like ships that pass in the night.'

'Surely not.' She could hardly speak. Was there glass in her throat?

'Women have always seen me as a good catch. Rich women, women looking for a man with the right-sized bank balance, who thought that if they agreed to everything I asked they could eventually get me to agree to putting that gold band around their finger. I enjoyed their company, but I was never tempted to settle down.' He paused. 'Open the box.'

She opened it. There was a ring there, nestled on a bed of black velvet. A gold band with two diamonds entwined on the top. She stared at it, feeling sick, hating herself for what she had to do and hating Fate for giving her this glimpse of happiness which she knew could never be hers.

'You're different from the rest of them, Katherine Lewis. You're genuine.'

No! she wanted to shout at him. No, I'm not!

'I can't accept this, Dominic.' I love you, she thought,

and love has made me strong and made me weak at the same time. Will you ever understand that? No, of course you won't. I can hardly understand it myself. It's a new world and one with which I'm unfamiliar.

'You think you need time? Is that it? I feel as though I've known you forever.' He was frowning.

'That's not it.' Her grey eyes were wide and miserable. 'I just can't, that's all.'

'I don't accept that,' he told her, not taking the box, in fact not paying the slightest bit of attention to it whatsoever. 'You must have known that I was falling in love with you.'

In a perfect world, she thought. But she could hardly complete the thought, because it wasn't a perfect world. In a perfect world there would be no tears and no regrets, no words to be uttered that were so hard that every syllable tore at your soul.

'We aren't meant for each other,' she whispered.

'You're talking rubbish,' he said tightly, and she could see that he was beginning to get angry, a dark, baffled anger that frightened her.

'Your world is somewhere else,' she said, struggling to tell him the truth without telling him all of it. She could tell him that she had been living a lie for the past six months, but then that would drag her down into a quagmire of questions, none of which she could answer. The truth, as it stood, was too awful for words. The truth, as it stood, had given her the wild courage to be someone she never had been, but now it forced her to be a monster.

'Of course,' he said, and his expression cleared, 'my home is in France, but naturally we wouldn't be living there all year. We could spend six months there and six months in London.' He threw her a crooked, amused smile. 'George would be only too grateful. He says that most of the time he feels as though he's hibernating, looking after an apartment that's only used a couple of times a year. This problem is not insurmountable.'

Katherine didn't say anything. The box with the ring was burning her hands.

'The country has nothing to do with this,' she told him. 'I just can't accept it. I just can't marry you, Dominic.'

She had never imagined that he would fall in love with her. He was, Emma had told her, a notorious heart-breaker. He would give her a good, uncomplicated time, and Katherine had been so sure that she had not had the where-withal to captivate a man like him that she had closed her eyes and let herself be led. Open me up, she had said, handing him the key, and he had, and it was only in the past few days that she had realised that in turning the key to her heart he had changed himself. Or perhaps she had just been blind all along. Blind and, underneath the glamorous wrapping, still the same insecure person she thought that she had left behind, too insecure to believe that the impossible had happened.

'I see.' Coldness was beginning to creep into his voice and she could see the shutter coming down over his eyes.

'No, you don't,' she said pleadingly. She held out the box and he threw it a scathing look.

'I think I understand perfectly, Katherine,' he said with glacial politeness. 'You've been having a good time but not quite good enough to warrant a commitment.' He stood up and began walking away and she followed, half running to keep up with him.

'Please stop, Dominic,' she called, trying to keep her voice low and not draw too much attention to what was going on.

He stopped, looked at her and said in a hard voice, 'Why? So that we can talk? I can't stand people who waste time performing post-mortems on a relationship.' Then he moved on, and she walked alongside him, still half running, because his long legs covered the distance so much more easily than hers.

'I can't keep this,' she told him. 'You must take your ring back. It must have cost you a fortune.'

'It did,' he said smoothly, stopping to look down at her. All the warm charm which she had seen in the past had vanished, replaced by a cold calm that terrified her.

She had always known that he was a hard man, that underneath the surface was a layer of steel. She had witnessed it a couple of times, in his dealings with people whom he disliked. He would talk to them, but there would always be something forbidding in his voice, a reminder that there were lines beyond which they were not allowed to step.

'There's only one law when it comes to business,' he had once told her, smilingly serious. 'It's the law of the jungle. I play fair, but if someone tries to cross me, it's only right that I should make it crystal-clear who's boss.'

'I have no need for it,' he said to her now, with a smile on his face that sent a little shiver of apprehension down her spine. 'Keep it. Let it be a souvenir for you, a scalp to go on your belt.'

'You don't understand,' Katherine mumbled, fidgeting from one foot to the other, unwilling to let him go like this, but equally unwilling to face the truth that she had no choice.

'I suppose,' he said, with the same dangerous smile on his face, and choosing to ignore her plea, 'that I should be grateful. At least you weren't a gold-digger. You never accepted anything from me. At the time I found that enchanting. There are very few rich men who aren't beguiled by a woman to whom money apparently means nothing.'

'No, your money never meant a thing to me.' There, at least, she could be honest.

He shoved his hands in his pockets and looked steadily at her. He had amazing eyes. A peculiar, deep shade of green. Eyes that glittered; eyes that could stare at her and through her, down into depths she had never known existed. Or so it had seemed.

'Were you interested in something else?' he asked softly. 'Were you only interested in proving to yourself that you could conquer a man like me?'

'No, of course not!' she denied feverishly. 'How could you think that?'

'What I'm looking for here, Katherine, are a few answers. Won't you be a good girl and oblige?'

Her heart was racing inside her. She could feel it. Hammering away like a steam-engine, making her breathless and unsteady. Very slowly she sat down on the nearest bench, partly because she knew that if she didn't she would collapse, and partly because, if she sat down, she wouldn't have to look at him. She could focus her attention somewhere else. There was a lake of sorts a few yards away and she concentrated on it.

On the opposite side of the water there was a mother with two young children. The children were having a ball, standing as close to the water as they could feasibly get, and their mother looked on anxiously, ready to leap forward the minute one of them fell in. Katherine watched the antics and didn't turn when Dominic sat down next to her. She could feel him, though, every vibration emanating from that hard, masculine body.

'I know you must think that I don't care, but I do,' she said, looking straight ahead of her. Care, she thought—what an inappropriate word to describe what I feel for you, every nuance of every emotion which fills me up and makes me whole.

'How generous of you.'

'But I still can't marry you. I shall never be able to marry you. I should never have become involved with you in the first place.'

That was true as well. At the beginning she had been too thrilled to pay much attention to the consequences of her actions. In a dark world he had been a sudden, blinding ray of light, and she had been drawn to the source of the light like a moth to a flame. Everything so new, so wonderful, all happening to *her*, unextraordinary little *her* whose plainness had been drummed into her from the time she was old enough to understand.

'You'll never amount to anything,' her mother had used to say to her. 'You're too plain, my girl. Like your father. I could have had anyone, but I chose him, and look at what he did to me.'

She had known from a very early age that her resemblance to her father was a crime for which she would never be forgiven, and her mother had reminded her of it so often that eventually Katherine had learnt how to switch off when the subject was raised.

Dominic had brought her alive. He had seen her, and she had blossomed under those clever, sexy, watchful green eyes.

'Why not?' he asked sharply. 'Why shouldn't you have become involved with me?'

'I had no right. It was selfish.'

'Stop talking in riddles. If you have something to say, then why don't you come right out and say it?'

'We're not suited,' she said helplessly.

'That's rubbish.'

'We're not alike.'

'I don't want a mirror image of myself. I'm not a narcissist.'

'That's not what I'm saying!' She was beginning to lose the thread of her logic now. She should have just let it go, let him walk off, but something in her wanted to leave him with feelings that weren't all bad. Was that selfish too?

'I'm not a glamorous person,' she attempted, meaning it. She wasn't. She had had her stab at glamour; she had borrowed Emma's clothes and worn them with her hair down and she had enjoyed it, but it wasn't her. Her flamboyance was born of fear and desperation, a need to see it all before the opportunity slipped between her fingers. She was the person who squeezed her eyes tightly and then parachuted down to earth. The people below might think her brave and only she would know her private terror.

The woman he had fallen in love with had been a chimera, an illusion, someone she had created for reasons which she could not reveal.

'You're an extremely glamorous person, Katherine Lewis,' he said, turning to face her, and she made sure that she kept her profile firmly averted.

'You need someone else. What you think you've found in me, you haven't.' There she went again, she thought, making a muddle of it, trying to say so much but not too much.

'Stop telling me what sort of woman I want,' he said, his voice like a whip. 'I don't want to sit here and listen to flimsy excuses. You've told me that you won't marry me and what I want to know is why. I don't want a damned dissertation on compatibility.'

'Life isn't black and white!' she snapped, getting angry. She stopped looking at the two children, whose mother had finally given in to anxiety and was dragging them away from the lake with vague promises about coming back another day.

'When?' the older of the two was asking in a high voice. 'Another day, *when?*'

'Another day, some time soon! Now, stop complaining. If you stop complaining, I'll buy you both an ice-cream.'

They promptly shut up. How wonderful, Katherine thought, to be a child, to have problems sorted out with ice-cream cones.

'It is,' Dominic said harshly, 'when it comes to something like this. I asked you to marry me, you said no, and I want to know why.'

'Haven't you ever been refused anything in your life before?' Katherine threw at him.

'Not very often and never by a woman.'

'Well, aren't you the lucky one?' She could feel the wall between them getting higher and higher, and she wished that she had chosen the coward's way out and left him a note. She might have done too, except that she had a suspicion that he would have ripped it into a thousand pieces and hunted her down until he found her. If only to drag answers out of her.

'Tell me!' he roared, and Katherine felt passing relief that the two children had vanished. They would have been instantly startled into falling into the lake otherwise.

'What do you want me to tell you?' she shouted back angrily.

Anger made it easier. It took over from pain; it took over from fantasising that the truth would make him feel anything other than hatred or pity.

'I want to know if you're walking out on me because of another man!'

'If that's what you want me to tell you, then I'll say it!' she flung back at him, and his face darkened with rage. He gripped her shoulders with his hands, and she could feel his fingers pushing down into her skin, hurting her.

'Yes!' he snarled. 'Let me hear you say it!'

'All right, then, fine! The reason I can't marry you is because of another man. Satisfied?'

As soon as the words were out, she regretted saying them. She half opened her mouth to deny it all, but he didn't give her the opportunity.

'Eminently satisfied,' he fired. 'Did you do it to make him jealous? Did it work, Katherine?'

'You made me say that,' she told him, and all the old feelings of hopeless misery were creeping back again. Her anger had dissipated as quickly as dew in the hot sun. She very rarely lost her temper. Living with her mother all those years had built up a layer of silent self-control. Words spoken in the heat of the moment, she had discovered from an early age, were the most wounding and the most difficult to retract.

'In a way, I'm glad I met you,' he said, standing up, and there was a stillness about his movements that was as alarming as the black fury on his face had been earlier on. 'I've learnt a valuable lesson from you. Deception isn't always obvious.'

Katherine scrambled to her feet, and when she met his eyes she saw the scathing dislike there.

Now there was nothing left to say. She had done what she had to do, but, as things had turned out, she had achieved it in the worst possible way.

'Here,' she said, handing him the box. 'Take it. Please.'

He reached out, and for a second his fingers brushed against hers. How painful to think that this, the last time he touched her, it would be with hatred and bitter disillusionment.

His fingers closed around the box and he flung it into

the water. There was cold satisfaction on his lips when he looked at her.

'Some things are better buried, don't you think?'

Then he turned and walked away. She followed him with her eyes all the way until he disappeared from sight, then she sat back down and stared at the pond. All her dreams were lying there at the bottom. The ring that would never be hers, and, the love which she had been compelled to reject.

She only stirred when it began to get chilly and the park started emptying of people.

Then she made her way back to Emma's flat, packed her suitcase, left a note and headed for the station. She would call her friend in the morning and explain what had happened, but omitting the details.

Better this way, she kept telling herself. In many ways, better for him. She kept thinking that all the way back to her home town.

Better for him to leave her with an anger he could understand. Nebulous reasons, however true they were for her, would have not been a clean break for him. How would he ever have understood that she wasn't the woman he thought she was? Would he have accepted it as easily as the thought of another man?

Her house was waiting there for her, patient and faithful. Katherine stood on the path up to the front door and sighed.

I did what I did for myself to start with, she said silently in her head, shutting her eyes. But in the end I did what I did for you.

How could you have coped with the truth? How could you have coped with the fact that I'm dying? Would you have felt betrayed or would you have felt obliged to stay with me through pity? Wouldn't either have been more destructive than the way I took?

She opened her eyes, raised her hand and, without thinking about it, coiled her hair into a ponytail, then went inside.

CHAPTER TWO

CHAPTER TWO

KATHERINE looked around her at the roomful of bright,
young faces. Outside, the warm sunshine spilled over the
green playing-fields, poured through the open windows and
generally helped to propagate the illusion that maybe, this
year, winter would hibernate to another country.

September was always lovely. New term, a few new
faces, back to work after the long summer holidays. Every
year the holidays loomed in front of her, waiting to be
filled, threatening to depress if they weren't, and she was
always glad to get back. Back to the sanctuary of her teaching. Away from thoughts of events that had happened six
long years ago. Six years! So long ago that she was vaguely
ashamed that the memory of them could still plague her
with such force, especially when time hung heavy on her
hands and there were no demands of work to keep her mind
in its harness.

There were two new girls. Victoria, who seemed to have
settled in already in the space of a few hours, helped by
the fact that she already knew some of the children in the
class, and Claire, small, dark-haired, with far too grave an
expression on her face for a child of barely five.

Katherine introduced them both to the rest of the class,
all girls, and briefly contemplated the dark-haired addition.
She would have to take this one under her wing. She could
spot at a glance those little pupils who would need over
and above the average attention. Usually they were the

quiet ones who, left on their own, would easily retreat into their natural shyness.

This little one, she thought, was far too serious, anxious, even, and quite handicapped by the fact that her first language was French, so much of the good-natured chattering of the rest of the girls was literally incomprehensible to her.

The good thing was that the girl would, at least, be at the start of the learning curve, only slightly behind the other girls who were largely *au fait* with simple reading. She smiled, touched the neat little bun pinned at the back of her neck, and began class.

'What do you know about her?' Katherine asked a week later, when she was in the staff-room with Jane Ray, the head of the preparatory school.

Jane Ray was a small, capable woman with short dark hair and darting black eyes, largely hidden behind a pair of spectacles. Katherine found it very easy to talk to her. She and the other teachers appreciated the way they were generally left to their own devices, free to implement their teaching in whatever imaginative methods they found the best.

'Not a great deal,' Jane admitted. 'She came to the open day at Easter, quite desperate for a place here because of a company move of some kind or another, but I couldn't extract very much background information. She was being dragged from room to room by a young woman, her nanny in France, I gathered, who either didn't speak any English or, from the looks of it, had decided to conceal the fact that she did. Lived in France all her life, somewhere near Paris, I gather. Never been to school before. Why?'

Katherine shrugged, frowning. 'She looks as though she's carrying the weight of the world on her shoulders.'

'You shouldn't worry overmuch about that,' Jane

laughed, but her dark eyes rested on Katherine thoughtfully. 'Children adapt far more easily than adults expect. By next week Claire Laudette will be well on her way to settling in. Even the language barrier will cease to be a problem. Have you ever noticed how children communicate? It's all hands and expression at that age!' They laughed, and Jane continued seriously, 'Your problem will be that you'll leave this school in the afternoon and you'll take your worries about Claire home with you, and you mustn't do that.'

'I shan't!' Katherine protested. 'I don't!'

'I'll speak honestly, Katherine. I worry about you sometimes.'

There was a little silence. Katherine dreaded it when people decided to speak honestly to her. She knew how her life must appear to outsiders. Calm, placid, a lovely job, but lacking in excitement.

'Do you mean that I'm not doing my job properly?' she asked, deliberately misreading the statement, and Jane shook her head.

'Oh, no, we were delighted when you reapplied for your job here after your six months away. You're an extremely good teacher. You stimulate the children, get them interested in the basics—no, I can't fault that.' She sighed. 'You know what I mean, don't you?'

'I'm happy.' Katherine looked down at her fingers. Yes, I am happy, she told herself. I have a roof over my head, a job I enjoy, friends—what else could I ask for? In her more optimistic moments, she even tried to convince herself that in time she would be able to put that disastrous episode behind her. It couldn't haunt her for the rest of her life, could it?

She should, she knew, be grateful that she had been given this second chance at life. She could still remember the private anguish of thinking that she was living on borrowed time, just as clearly as she could remember her dizzy, weak euphoria when she had returned to her cottage all that time ago and found that letter on her doormat, sandwiched between the usual circulars and out-of-date bills. The letter that had informed her politely about the confusion with her notes, apologised courteously for an error of mistaken identity, informed her gaily that she was perfectly healthy. Too late for her, of course, but, yes, she had told herself, I am grateful and I am happy, and she had continued telling herself that as time passed.

'Perhaps I'll give little Claire a bit of private tuition. Just a few minutes after class. She isn't collected until four.'

'I'm sure that would be very helpful,' Jane said with a resigned smile, 'but you mustn't forget that you have a life of your own to live.'

Have I? Katherine would have liked to ask. Living, she thought, truly living, was something that entailed joy and despair, hopes and dreams and all the ups and downs that gave life its pleasing tempo.

Her life, when she thought about it, was like the flat, undisturbed, glassy surface of a pond. She was content, but she knew that contentment was not what Jane was talking about.

'I won't,' she said dutifully, and that was the end of that. She had become adept at skirting around the details of her private life. She went to the movies, had meals out with her small circle of friends, read a lot, busied herself with her work, but her feelings and emotions she kept to herself.

It was as if, she frequently thought, those heady six months had never really existed. She could hardly believe that she had ever stretched her wings like that and flown free, although she remembered the pain of the landing as bitterly and as clearly as if it had all happened yesterday, and not six long years ago.

She was now no longer a girl. That was something she faced without flinching. She was in her thirties, almost thirty-two, and destined, she knew, to be on her own forever more. That was something she didn't like to think about too hard. Forever. What a lonely ring that had to it.

The following day she began spending time after school with Claire. In the past week she had discovered that the child's reserve had nothing to do with her intelligence. Claire Laudette was extremely bright.

They sat side by side in the empty classroom, and it was only when an elderly lady came in that Katherine realised that the few minutes which she had allocated to helping with reading had stretched into a full hour.

I won't make this a habit, she told herself that evening. I'll do as much as I can during the school day and then, occasionally, I'll stay after class until her English has improved.

But there was something curiously vulnerable about the girl, and it touched something equally vulnerable in Katherine.

Little by little, over a period of a few weeks, she also began learning snippets of information about Claire's home life and, much as she disliked her curiosity, she found herself becoming more and more interested in Claire Laudette as a little person, as opposed to Claire Laudette as a pupil and nothing more.

'I have no mother and Papa is never at home,' she would say, apropos nothing in particular. 'We do not have any pets. He does not allow animals.' This didn't seem to bother her in the slightest, but it bothered Katherine.

'He does not like me to trouble him,' she would say casually, or, 'Papa does not have much time for me,' and the picture that began building in Katherine's head was so alarming that she began to think about arranging to see him one evening.

She knew all about the damage an uncaring parent could do to a child. Hadn't she suffered the slings of that when she was young?

'What about the lady who comes to collect you from school?' Katherine asked gently. 'She looks very nice. Is she your aunt, perhaps?'

'Papa pays her.' Claire was busy colouring a picture she had drawn, a crooked house with lop-sided windows and disproportionately large flowers huddled on one side. 'He says that money can buy anything.'

Katherine sent the note home with the child that evening. It was short and to the point. She wanted to see Claire's father and, rather than leave it to him to arrange a time, she suggested one. That way, he would have to make an effort to cancel the time she suggested or else he would come along. She hadn't yet worked out what she intended to say to this man, but she would let her intuition guide her. She could usually tell a great deal about the parents from the children, anyway.

The aggressive ones, who were prone to bullying if allowed to get away with it, tended to have socially aggressive parents, mothers who spent a fortune on their clothes and managed to persuade their little angels, without actually saying so in so many words, that they were superior to everyone else.

From what she had seen of Clair Laudette, and from what she had gleaned, she had already formed a very clear impression of her father. A strident man, too selfish to care about his offspring, driven by a need to stack up piles of money, who probably drank. She could imagine him storming through the house, his face ill-tempered, while his daughter cowered away somewhere in a bedroom. A child who seldom laughed, she thought, thinking back to her own silent childhood, rarely had anything to laugh about.

She had arranged to see him that evening at six at the school, and she had persuaded Jane to let her use her office for the meeting.

'I shall be seeing your daddy this evening,' she told Claire as the child was getting ready to leave, and the worried look, which had been absent for a while, settled on her face.

'Why?' she asked anxiously, chewing on her bottom lip and frowning. 'You won't say anything bad about me, will you?' she asked with a tremor in her voice, and Katherine said huskily,

'Of course not!' She gave a bright smile. 'A bright little thing like you? No, I just want to tell him how wonderfully you're getting along. I'm sure he wants to know.'

In fact, she had dressed specially for the purpose of telling him just how well his daughter was doing, and dropping a few hints about the importance of parental support in a child's life.

Warm though it was, she had worn her navy blue suit with a crisp white shirt underneath, and she would make sure that her long hair was pinned very tightly back from her face, no loose strands anywhere.

In six years she had let her hair grow, and it now reached almost to her waist. Soon she would have to have it cut. Long hair at her age was a bit inappropriate, but she didn't look like a woman in her early thirties. She knew that. She might be plain, but her face was unlined and her grey eyes were clear. Her friends had stopped telling her that the lines would develop quickly enough, just as soon as she had a couple of children. Marriage and children were subjects which they tactfully avoided now that it looked as though neither was on the horizon.

At five to six she began wondering whether she should meander out to the entrance to wait for him. At five past six she decided not to, and at ten past, when she was beginning to wonder whether he would make an appearance at all, she looked up and saw him standing in front of her, his body outlined in the doorway of the office.

And he was precisely as she remembered him. He was even holding his jacket over his shoulder, exactly as he had done all those years ago as he had walked across to her in Regent's Park.

She opened her mouth in shock and half rose out of the chair, feeling as though at any minute she would faint. The room felt close, as though there wasn't enough air in it, making her dizzy, disorientated. She had to place her palms on the desk to support herself.

'You!' It was the only form of greeting she was capable of. If he was as shocked as she was, then he recovered quickly, moving towards her with the same graceful, economic stride she remembered.

'Katherine Lewis,' he said without smiling. His eyes were hard and shuttered.

'I had no idea that you were Claire's father,' she said, finding her voice at last, and not managing to say what she wanted.

'Nor,' he said coolly, 'did I think for a minute that the Miss Lewis whom my daughter talks about incessantly was none other than you.' He paused, and his eyes raked her up and down with dislike. 'What an unpleasant surprise for both of us.'

The memories of him were rushing over her, but that dislike in his eyes restored some of her balance, and she sat down again, indicating to him the chair facing her across the desk.

She could feel her heart beating wildly in her chest, like a trapped, fluttering bird wanting escape.

She had collected some of Claire's work. It lay in front of her in a neat little pile and she rested her hand on it, hoping that it would remind her what the purpose of this meeting was, but she could feel Dominic's hard eyes straying over her, and she didn't have to try too hard to imagine what he was thinking.

Was this the same girl he had known all those years ago? This ageing woman with the neatly pinned hair and the severe suit? She felt momentarily unbalanced by the inspection and had to remind herself that this was one of the reasons why she had walked out on him in the first place. Because this was her, the last sort of person he would find attractive. More the sort of woman he would probably pity.

'Unpleasant or not, the fact stands that I am Claire's teacher—' she cleared her throat '—and I called you in to see me so that we could discuss what your daughter has been doing.'

She had never really imagined that he would marry. In her mind, he had remained the startlingly attractive bachelor whom she had known, but, really, it would have been unusual if he hadn't married.

Had he loved his wife? she wondered. What had happened to her? Were they divorced?

'I have some of Claire's work here,' she said, staring down at the little bundle of papers with their childish drawings and round, uneven writing.

'You've changed.'

'Everyone changes,' Katherine said sharply, but his words flustered her badly. 'It's the effect of time.'

'So you're now a teacher, of all things.'

'That's right. Now, shall we discuss your daughter or

would you like to spend a bit more time denigrating me? I'm a busy woman, Mr Duvall.'

'Are you? Busy doing what? No wedding-ring on your finger, so I take it that you're not married?'

She was feeling more and more addled, like a mouse being toyed with by a cat, confusedly running round and round, looking for somewhere to hide.

'I've got some things that your daughter has done.' She handed the stack of work to him and he took it, flicking through the papers, holding them in different directions so that he could interpret the drawings. Katherine watched his lowered head and thought that, if she had changed, he certainly hadn't. It hardly seemed fair that six years could have had so little physical impact on him. His dark looks were just as disturbing as they had been, his body still as lithe and hard. Her eyes strayed to his fingers—long, clever fingers. She briefly closed her eyes and tried not to think back to the feel of those fingers on her body.

He had taken her body once, and he had kept it. She had known no other lover but him, although there were men in her life now. Friends. Harmless, good-natured men, who were husbands of her friends, and David, another schoolteacher, though not at her school. David was harmless and good-natured too and, given half a chance, he would have progressed their friendship on to a far more intimate level. But ever since Dominic... It wasn't fair, she thought with a burst of angry rebellion. His life had moved on—he had married, produced a beautiful child. Emotionally, and this was the first time she had acknowledged this to herself, her life had stagnated, like a clock that had stopped ticking.

He was looking at her, his eyes guarded, watchful, and she forced herself to resume her efficient, businesslike air.

'What am I supposed to say about these?' he asked, depositing the stack of papers on the desk and reclining in the chair.

'Most parents express delight at their children's efforts,' Katherine informed him, keeping her voice even. 'Work-wise, Claire has settled very nicely into class. Was she at school before you came here?'

'No.' His voice did not encourage interested debate on the subject.

'I see. She seems to have a very good grasp of English, in that case. Her knowledge of the alphabet is excellent, and she is quite a fluent reader, considering.'

'Considering what?'

'Considering,' she said, with two angry patches of colour on her cheeks, 'that this is her first brush with school.'

'Her mother was bilingual.' His voice was flat and ex-pressionless and gave no insight into what he thought of this bilingual woman.

'I see.' She paused, alarmed by his hostility, and ner-vously touched the tightly coiled bun at the back of her neck. 'I do feel, however,' she continued, 'that children, especially at Claire's age, need a great deal of parental input. I gather that your wife is not here at the moment?'

'And from whom have you gleaned that piece of infor-mation?' he asked coldly. 'I hope you haven't been quiz-zing my daughter on her private life, because I can't say that I see what Claire's home life has to do with her work, and you tell me that her work is entirely satisfactory.'

'This is a school, Mr Duvall,' Katherine informed him with equal coolness. 'We do not make it a habit to inter-rogate our pupils. However, what happens in a child's home has a great deal of bearing on what happens in school. Claire is very reserved, very anxious.'

'And you're somehow blaming me for that?' He shot her a look of scathing dislike.

'I'm not blaming you for anything,' she responded acidly. She had never before dealt with a difficult parent. In general, parents who paid for their children's education took an inordinate delight in their progress. At parent-teacher evenings, they would hang on to her every word.

Dominic Duvall could not have been more unhelpful if he'd tried, and she knew that personal dislike of her would be playing a part in that, though to what extent she had no idea.

'Let's get one thing very clear from now,' he said, leaning forward slightly, and his presence was so overwhelming that she felt herself press back into her chair. 'Neither you nor anyone else has any business prying into my personal life. Your job here is to educate my daughter, and that's where your duty ends.'

'And the fact that we once knew each other has no bearing on what you're saying now?' Katherine asked, stirred into making the remark through sheer anger at his attitude. 'Please don't let your dislike for me colour your reactions to what I've been telling you.'

'Spare me your schoolmistress speech,' he snarled, his mouth tight. 'What happened between us is in the past. If I hadn't decided to send my daughter to this school, we would never have crossed paths again. The fact that we have, my dear Miss Lewis, is unfortunate, but it's something we both have to live with. In the meantime, please do not interest yourself in my daughter's home life.' He stood up. The meeting, as far as he was concerned, was at an end, and Katherine hastily followed suit, crossly knowing that control had been taken out of her hands.

They went out into the assembly-room, where a group of older children were doing ballet. The piano teacher was banging impatiently on the keys while a handful of girls frowningly concentrated on trying to get their feet into some kind of synchronisation.

Dominic stopped and looked around him with interest, then his eyes flicked across to her.

'What made you decide to give up your job in advertising?' he asked, sticking his hands in his pockets and moving on, expecting her to hurry behind him but, she gathered from his attitude, not much caring whether she did or didn't.

She had to think a bit about what he had said, then she remembered that a job in advertising had all been part of the myth which she had created for herself during those short, heady months of another life.

'I enjoy teaching,' she answered awkwardly. 'And what have you been doing for the past six years?'

They went out into the hall, where some more girls were sitting on the ground, cross-legged, waiting to be collected. Behind them, the wall was one large notice-board—listing school events, displaying paintings done by some of the pupils.

Judith Evans, one of the teachers, was sitting by the doors, trying to keep one eye on the girls while correcting homework. She looked at Katherine, then slid her eyes across to Dominic with great interest.

'Working,' he said smoothly, opening the door and stepping outside.

Katherine hesitated, then she stepped out behind him, letting the door shut behind her.

'Claire mentions that she doesn't see a great deal of you,' she began, and he turned on her, his green eyes filled with distaste.

'I thought that we'd been through all this,' he said in a hard voice, and Katherine stuck her chin out defensively.

'You've been through all this, Mr Duvall. However, just

because you've decided on what's important in Claire's life and what isn't, it doesn't mean that I have agreed.'

He looked her up and down unhurriedly, then said, 'And you are the final word on what's best for a child, are you? Tell me, have you any children of your own?'

'No,' she admitted in a low voice, lowering her eyes. 'But I really don't see what that has to do with it. I have a great deal of experience with children in general.'

'No children,' he mused, with enough thick irony in his voice to make her flush with anger. 'No husband. What happened to the misguided lover?'

She didn't have to think too hard about that one. She remembered the fictitious lover whom she had hurled at Dominic when he had demanded a reason from her, a reason for leaving.

'That's none of your business,' she muttered, looking away and staring at the playing-fields, where more girls were playing hockey in the distance.

It had never struck her before, but now she thought, how strange, to surround myself with children, children who represent everything that I no longer have—hopes, dreams, a life ahead to be filled with everything I shall never be able to attain.

Would Dominic Duvall ever know just how successfully he had wrecked her life? She would never forgive him for that, even though she knew that the fault for it all lay in her own hands, because she should never have become involved with him in the first place. Not in the way that she had, not fuelled by motives which had seemed so right at the time, but in the end had proved so misguided.

'Did the grand reconciliation never take place?' he asked, sarcastic and amused, which made her even angrier. 'Poor little Katherine Lewis. Or maybe you're one of those ever-hopeful women, still walking along the garden path, opti-

mistically thinking that she'll get her man in the end, if
only she can hold out for long enough.' He laughed under
his breath, a cruel, jeering sound. 'Is he still holding out
the promises he made to get you back?' he asked, looking
down at her with a smile that was as hard as ice.

'This is irrelevant,' Katherine said, trying to sound brisk
and instead only managing to sound defensive.

'Oh, but I'm merely trying to piece you together. Natural
human curiosity. You asked me about what I'd been doing
over the past six years. Well, I'm merely speculating on
what you've been doing.'

'I must get back to the school,' she said, turning away,
but before she could walk off she felt his fingers snap
around her arm.

'What for?' he asked, raising his eyebrows. 'To tidy
desks?'

'You may think that what I do is boring,' she snapped,
'but teaching is as essential as what you do. A person's
usefulness in life isn't judged by the amount of money they
earn. And kindly remove your hand from me.'

He removed his hand and she drew back, aware with
horror that she was shaking like a leaf.

'Dear me,' he said, coolly amused, 'I do hope my questions haven't upset you.'

'You hope nothing of the sort, Mr Duvall. And, no, your
questions haven't upset me. They've annoyed me.'

She fervently wished that that were the case, but she
knew that she was deeply unbalanced by this sudden appearance in her life of the one man whose image she had
spent years trying to erase.

'Do you normally tremble when you're annoyed?' he
asked, politely curious.

'No,' she answered icily, 'I don't. Perhaps it's just that
you were the last person in the world I expected or wanted

to confront. No one likes to be reminded of past mistakes, do they?'

His lips thinned and she had to steel herself not to take a step backwards. Had she forgotten how threatening he could be? His green eyes could assume the wintry, terrifying depths of the ocean, and that leashed power which always hovered so close to the surface reminded her that he was not a man to be crossed.

'Least of all when they've learnt nothing from them,' he countered with dangerous calm. 'Did your lover hold out promises to you on condition that you buried yourself here, teaching? Tell me, what makes a woman give up a life of excitement in exchange for the sedate, the unthreatening?'

Of course, she had always suspected that her real life would arouse only his contempt, but hearing him say so made her stiffen.

'Is he worth it? You must introduce me to him.'

'I happen to like it here,' she said evenly. 'And since you feel so free to ask me questions about my private life, you won't mind if I ask you a few about your own? How long did you wait after we broke up before you married?'

'Would you like to hear that I gave our dead relationship a suitable period of mourning?' He laughed aloud at that. 'I met Françise six weeks after I left London and I married her two months later. Disappointed?'

'What happened to her?'

There was a thick silence, which only lasted seconds but was long enough for her to wonder whether anger had pushed her into asking something which really was none of her business. She wished that she had not asked; she wished that she had simply walked off. The last thing she wanted to do was reveal to him the depth of her interest in his life, reawakened after so long a slumber.

'Franqise was involved in a fatal accident nine months ago,' he said abruptly.

'I'm so sorry.'

'How kind of you,' he grated.

'I meant it! It must have been very hard on Claire, and on you as well.' Was this why he appeared so bitter at the mention of his ex-wife's name? The deepest pain, she knew, was the pain caused when love was prematurely extinguished. She tried not to contemplate the hurtful fact that that ring, still lying at the bottom of that pond in Regent's Park for all she knew, had been the mistake which he had rectified.

'I don't think that strolling down memory lane is serving any purpose, do you?' he asked, and the mask of cool self-control had settled back on his face. 'You say that Claire is doing well, but is she keeping up with the other children?'

Relieved that they were once again back on home ground, she visibly relaxed and began to discuss Claire's progress.

She was accustomed to talking about children and their performance at school. It was a subject with which she felt comfortable. She only realised that they were strolling back to the car park when she found herself standing next to a black BMW. By which time she had regained all of her lost self-control, and could actually lift her eyes to Dominic's face without that numbing loss of composure which she had experienced earlier on. She even managed to smile, which was something she considered quite a feat, given the circumstances.

'I tend to get a little carried away when it comes to discussing the children,' she heard herself say in a very normal voice, the sort of voice she would have used for any parent, half apologetic, half amused, wholly sincere.

'So I see.' There was speculation in his eyes and she wondered uneasily what he was thinking. 'Your career obviously suits you.'

'I like children,' Katherine said, in a voice which did not invite comment. 'Why did you decide to move to the Midlands?' she asked, changing the subject.

He pulled open the car door and paused.

'Because, next to London, Birmingham has the most potential for my company,' he said, and she could tell from his manner that he was still speculating about her, trying to match up the two halves of the personality which he had seen.

'All part of the master plan to conquer the world?' she asked lightly, and for the first time, when he laughed, there was none of that metallic edge to his laughter.

'I have to fill my time somehow,' he said, his eyes still intent on her face, and for reasons which she could not explain to herself she felt in real danger now. She didn't want to be reminded of that lethal charm beneath the aggression. That was even more disturbing than the bitter dislike.

She folded her arms and said nervously, 'Well, I must get back now. If there's anything you wish to discuss about Claire's work, then do feel free to contact me.' She backed away slightly from the car. 'After half-term, Mrs Gall, who's been off with appendicitis, will be returning, and there'll be a ballet option. You should have received a letter from the school about that.' He was still staring at her, and she felt herself getting hot and confused all over again.

'It's possible,' he said, with a shrug of his broad shoulders. 'I'm afraid I don't manage to keep track of all those letters.'

'I think she would enjoy it,' Katherine said lamely. 'It

might do her good to see some of the other children out of the classroom.'

'Fine.'

'Well.' She threw him an efficient smile. 'I do hope everything goes well with your business. This may not be London, but I'm sure you'll find the countryside just as pleasant.' She couldn't have been more bland if she had tried, even though she was quite sure that there was nothing he would find less appealing than rolling fields. He was not a man who would relish the peace that country life carried with it. He was too restless, too much a city animal. She wondered how long he would stay. Maybe just long enough for the subsidiary to be established, then he would return to the fast pace, the glamour, the constant demands of London or Paris or New York. Poor Claire. Would she become one of those children who were constantly transported around the world, who never tasted the roots of permanence? Or perhaps a lonely little child, sent to boarding-school because her father's career left no time to play at being a parent?

As she walked back to the school she heard the deep roar of the BMW as he started the engine, and she fought the temptation to look round.

He was back, she thought, but this was no grand reunion. There was too much bitterness, too many unspoken secrets flowing under this bridge.

She stopped to look at the girls playing hockey, remembering most of them from when they had been little four-year-olds, their minds waiting to be shaped, to be taught. This was her life and it had no room to house the past.

She stared at the running figures and wished, with a kind of quiet desperation, that the past had not caught up with her.

CHAPTER THREE

DAVID was saying something about departmental changes because of cut-backs, and at the same time worriedly attacking a piece of fish on his plate, as though it had something to do with what was happening at his school.

Katherine was only half listening to him. She couldn't really hear what he was saying anyway. The music was a little too insistent and her thoughts were wrapped up somewhere else.

For the past two weeks, ever since seeing Dominic, she had had the unfamiliar feeling of living on a knife's edge. She kept expecting him to surface at any moment to pick his daughter up, or else to discuss something with her, and every second that she was on the school premises had been spent in an agony of dreaded expectation.

Of course, he hadn't shown up, and it was only in the last few days that she could feel herself relaxing, although the relief which she should have felt at his non-appearance was not as immense as it should have been, and that in itself frightened her.

She looked down at her half-finished plate of pasta and tried to tune in to what David was telling her. Greg Thompson was going to be in line for assistant headmaster. She didn't know Greg Thompson, though, so she mumbled something unhelpful, some soothing, nondescript remark which could have been used for any number of conversations.

Poor David, she thought. He was the maths teacher at one of the local comprehensives and he lacked that ambitious edge which would have helped him overcome his deep suspicion that he was somehow unable to control his unruly classes. It constantly nagged away at him.

She looked at his kind, unassuming face, with its carefully cut brown hair and anxious brown eyes, and for the first time in years felt a certain amount of irritation. If the departmental changes bothered him so much, why on earth didn't he say something about it? But she knew better than to raise the issue with him. He was forever telling her that she had a cushy job, that teaching in a private school was leagues away from teaching in a state school.

'No get up and go,' her mother would have said. 'A born victim, that boy.' Her mother had been good at classifying people into categories. She used to tell her that she was one of life's victims, that she was destined to walk on the sidelines, until the day that she rebelled and did something disastrous.

'Cut in the same mould as your father,' she would say, with the overlying edge of certainty which did not invite argument. 'And look at what he did. I did everything for that man. I could have done better, but no, I stuck it out, married to a man who was never going to rise in life, and instead of being grateful, look at what he did—upped and left with a woman almost young enough to be his daughter.'

Was she a victim? She had fallen in love with a man who was too sophisticated for her, had put herself in a situation from which retreat had been painful and inevitable, and in so doing had condemned herself to a lifetime of wondering. What if things had been different? What if she had gone to London and had not been propelled for reasons that had been so complicated? What if she had stayed there? What if she had told him the truth? But no, that had never been an option. She had built their relationship on a personality which she had created, a convincing three-dimensional doll. No, the truth had never been an option, but what if...? What if...? She was here again, wrapped in the security of what she knew, but recently she could feel a disturbing restlessness in herself.

'You're not listening to a word I'm saying.' David pushed his plate aside and looked at her with a certain amount of pique. 'I'm boring you.'

'No! I'm very interested in what's going on at your school.' She looked at him with affection and applied her mind to the conversation at hand. 'Perhaps you should leave.'

'Leave and do what?' He sighed. 'Teaching is all that I'm cut out to do. That's like telling a fish to leave the water and try and make a life in a tree.'

Katherine grinned at him. 'You can be so descriptive,' she said. 'You're absolutely wasted teaching maths. You should give it all up and write a book.'

'You're mad,' he said, laughing, 'but maybe you're right. There's quite a lot to be said for getting out of school politics.' He sighed, and she noticed all the tell-tale signs of a man showing his age, even though he was only twenty-nine, younger than she was, in fact. There were small wrinkles around his eyes and mouth, and a sprinkling of grey hair in between the fine brown.

In an attempt to steer him away from more maudlin self-analysis, she began chatting about books, and was relieved when he took the cue.

She didn't feel that she could cope with David's problems, or anyone else's for that matter. She had enough of her own, and for once she decided that she would be selfish and not allow herself to become a never-ending sounding-board for other people. She had spent a lifetime listening to her mother and she had acquired a talent for listening, but the talent, she was discovering over the past few weeks, was not quite as accessible as it used to be. She couldn't bring herself to discuss her own problems with anyone else, she was too private a person for that, but neither could she bring herself to be the helpful ear that she once was.

It had only struck her recently that friends and colleagues took her availability for granted, and they always had.

They always knew where to find her; they always knew that she would be around if they were at loose ends or else had something to discuss.

Should she be flattered at that? she wondered. Or was it a reflection of some essential lack in her own life?

She frowned, leaving David to hold forth on the pleasant daydream of giving up the orthodox life for something more adventurous, and only snapped back to reality when her eyes, aimlessly drifting around the room, flitted over a tall, dark man standing by the bar with a drink in his hand.

She felt her heartbeat quicken and her mouth went dry.

The club, not the kind of place she normally frequented, was crowded and semi-dark. It was also loud. The owner, out to reap as much money as possible, had turned the place into restaurant, bar and disco. As far as Katherine was concerned, it was an unfortunate combination, because it ensured that none was quite good enough, but David had insisted, and she had not been able to come up with any valid reasons for not accompanying him.

Now she wished that she had stood her ground and found some excuse not to go, however lame.

She cringed back into her chair in an attempt to make herself invisible, and she would have succeeded if Dominic hadn't become fed up with the crush of people at the bar and decided to find somewhere quieter.

She watched him circle the dance-floor and make his way

across to where they were seated, although it was only when he was virtually on top of them that he saw them, by which time it was too late to stand up suddenly and pretend to be on the way out.

She saw the way his eyes flicked across to David, then back to her, with a sinking heart, and forced herself to smile with some semblance of a neutral welcome.

'Miss Lewis,' he said, speaking loudly to be heard over the din of the music. He turned to David, and said with a certain amount of lazy amusement in his voice, 'And you must be—'

'David Carr,' she cut in hurriedly, running through the introductions at the speed of light. 'We were just on the way out, actually.'

'Were we?' David looked at her with irritating bewilderment. 'I've still got a full glass here.'

'So you have,' Katherine mumbled lamely, horrified when David invited Dominic to join them.

'Why not?' he shrugged. 'But I'll have to pull another chair across. I'm here with a friend.' His voice was relaxed, pleasant, but every nerve in her body was attuned to the fact that there was something watchful about him, about the way his eyes slid over them, veiled, hidden, speculative.

He moved a chair across, which meant that they all had to shift their seating slightly, and she could feel his eyes on her as she re-adjusted her position and made an effort to view the situation with some degree of calm. She wouldn't let him rattle her like the last time. She could forgive herself for that—after all, the shock of seeing him again for the first time in six years would have thrown anyone—but their brief affair was now dead, and she would not let him see how much he still affected her.

She averted her face, took a sip from her glass, unfortunately only orange juice, so there wasn't much moral courage to be derived there, and crossed her legs.

She knew that she looked calm. In fact, she knew that she looked exactly what she was—a schoolteacher out for the night. Her flowered dress was loose and unadventurous, she was devoid of any make-up apart from some lipstick hurriedly applied as her one concession to vanity, and her long hair had been severely plaited down her back. She pulled the plait over her shoulder and nervously toyed with the end of it, twirling the hair in between her fingers.

David, thankfully, was maintaining some form of conversation, telling Dominic about his work, and she prayed that he wouldn't launch into his speech about the cut-backs.

I'll give it fifteen minutes, she thought firmly to herself, looking at David and pretending to be interested in what he was saying, and then I'll just stand up and leave. David would have no choice but to follow suit.

She glanced down at her watch, and when she raised her eyes Dominic's friend was at their table. A woman. What else had she expected?

'My friend, Jack,' Dominic said smoothly, taking his time. 'We've known each other for longer than I care to remember.' They exchanged a glance which spoke of a great deal of intimacy, and then the woman looked at them, with a slow grin and raised eyebrows.

Katherine stretched out her hand and tried hard to smile.

'My real name is Jacqueline,' she explained, in the same excellent but accented English as Dominic, 'but he refuses to call me anything but Jack until I grow my hair.'

She had very short, very dark hair and a supple body, loose-limbed and very graceful. She could well have been a ballerina if it hadn't been for her height. She was extremely tall, but her height, rather than making her look sophisticated, gave her a spectacularly appealing, gamine air.

She slipped into her chair and announced to no one in particular that she was having a marvellous time. Paris nightclubs had become boring. Too many beautiful people all trying to compete with one another. It was so small here. Were there any village halls? she wanted to know. Any village dances? She had read all about English village dances when she was a girl. They had always intrigued her. What, she wanted to know, did one wear to a village dance? What did one do, come to that, at a village dance? Was it all checked shirts and taking your partner by the hand? Her voice was breathless and engaging.

David appeared bemused, Dominic was looking at her, smiling with lazy indulgence, and Katherine sat back with a feeling of unbearable dowdiness.

'Claire talks about you all the time,' Jack said, smiling and turning to Katherine, then she said something very rapidly in French to Dominic and they both smiled. 'When I say "But what about the other little girls?" she says that she would prefer to invite you to tea.'

'A passing phase,' Katherine said in a very schoolmistressy voice. 'Once Claire settles in, she'll forget that I even exist.'

'And don't you find that rather frustrating?' Dominic asked in that deep, ironic voice. He reached out for his glass, drank, and then regarded her over the rim. 'Looking after children who move into your life for a short while, only to move out?'

'If I found it frustrating,' Katherine said stiffly, 'I wouldn't teach.'

Jack was looking at them, her eyes flitting between the two.

'You are not married?' she asked, and Katherine shook

her head with sudden embarrassment. 'Waiting for the right man to come along? Prince Charming, perhaps?'

'I hope not,' David said lightly. 'Where on earth would that leave me?'

At that, Jack launched into a confused metaphor about every Cinderella having her Prince Charming, at the end of which Dominic shook his head and murmured, amused, that she ought to steer clear of translating too many complicated idioms into English, 'Because, my sweet, it leaves you open to appearing rather foolish. Especially,' he added in a low drawl, 'in the presence of our little teacher here.' Which instantly made Katherine sound as though she spent her spare time analysing other people's grammar and correcting them.

'I think her English is rather impressive,' David said gallantly, though still wearing that bemused expression, as though he had suddenly found himself flying through space at the speed of light.

'I adore flattery,' Jack said, pouting and grinning at the same time. 'Come and dance with me. You don't mind, do you?' She looked at Katherine with an open smile. 'I don't want to be accused of snatching someone else's man away from them!'

They headed off to the dance-floor, threading their way through the crowds, and Dominic said, 'What do you think of her?'

'She seems very young and enthusiastic,' Katherine said, hating herself for sounding so horribly prim and proper, and then deciding that if he didn't like it he could lump it.

During those mad months in London she had been enthusiastic herself, she had dressed in daring clothes and said daring things, and had felt alive and vibrant. It seemed a lifetime away. It was a lifetime away.

'Dear me, you make that sound like a crime.'

'Stop laughing at me!' she snapped, looking at him angrily.

'I'm merely trying to work out,' he replied smoothly, 'how six years could have changed you into the person that you seem to be now. Scared, cautious, hiding behind starchy clothes and—' he glanced at her hair '—severe hair-styles.'

'I am not scared! Scared of what?'

'Life?'

'Just who do you think you are?' Katherine said unsteadily. 'You don't know me now and you didn't know me...then.'

'Didn't I?' He leaned forward. 'What makes you say that?'

'Stop badgering me!' She looked at the dark, clever face with alarm.

'Was I?' he asked in a bored voice, leaning back and looking around him. 'I thought that I was making civilised conversation. I take it that this David fellow was the man you felt obliged to run back to?' She could hear the cool dislike in his voice, although he wasn't looking at her.

'I've only known David for four years,' she said flatly.

'What happened to the other man? Did he decide that you weren't worth the candle?' He turned to look at her and, although his voice was only mildly interested, his eyes were sharp, intent.

'That's none of your business, and I refuse to discuss my private life with you.'

'Do you discuss it with anyone?' He pushed back his chair and crossed his legs, ankle resting lightly on knee.

'No, I don't,' she told him icily, 'and if I were to, believe me, you'd be bottom of the list as confidant.'

'What a defensive creature you've become,' he said, draining his glass, and she was tempted to inform him that she always had been defensive, that there were a thousand sides to her which he had not seen, and that the sides he had seen had never really existed.

He shrugged and linked his fingers together. 'Still, you can keep your secrets to yourself. You might like to know, however—' he looked across to the dance-floor, his eyes narrowing until he made out Jacqueline's figure next to David '—that I gave some thought to what you said about Claire, and Jack's going to be living with me to help out.'

'Is she?' Katherine felt a certain numbness spread through her at the thought of that and she shakily laughed at her foolishness. 'Did she not mind giving up Paris?'

'She's never been one to be averse to change.'

'No,' Katherine said stiffly. 'I'm surprised, though... She looks very young, and this is a very different cup of tea from Paris.'

'Jack is devoted to Claire.' When he said that his features softened and she felt a twinge of jealousy that was sharp enough to make her catch her breath. 'And she's not that young. Twenty-four, as a matter of fact, although she doesn't look her age.' There was fondness in his voice.

Katherine looked away. Twenty-four, she thought, and in love with life. Was it any wonder that he was smitten with her?

She thought of herself, and knew how she must appear to him—a laughable spinster, wrapped up in her little teaching job, finding fulfillment through other people's children—and she felt tears come briefly to her eyes.

'Claire must enjoy the company,' she said, blinking away the tears. She hated self-pity and she wasn't prone to it. She had taken too many knocks in life to be able to indulge in that particular trait. She had learnt from early on how to conceal her feelings and when, at night, she brought them out, they were for her eyes only.

'She does,' he said shortly. 'We both do. Jack is like a breath of fresh air.'

Katherine's eyes travelled to the dance-floor, where Jack and David were laughing during a lull in the music. Less than an hour before, she thought, David had been wallowing in worry. Now he looked as though he didn't have a care in the world.

They strolled towards them and the girl's face was animated. She was talking quickly, gesticulating a lot, and David was smiling and looking as though he had stumbled across some hitherto undiscovered, but delightful, alien form of being.

She went behind Dominic, slipped her arms around his neck and hugged him. Young, enthusiastic, vibrant. A breath of fresh air.

Katherine stood up, tugged at her flowered dress and announced that it was time to leave, forestalling any protests on David's part with a quelling look.

'So should we.' Dominic stood up and they made their way outside. They had to barge a path through the crowds, and by the time they were out in the open a heated debate had ensued between Dominic and Jack, who wanted to move on for a night-cap. In the semi-darkness outside the club she looked incredibly beautiful, utterly free, and petulant. David was sneaking little glances across to her, even though his hand was protectively on Katherine's arm.

'But why not?' she was protesting. 'Claire's safe and sound with the baby-sitter. What is the big hurry to get back to the house?'

She turned to them for support, so Katherine muttered, 'I'm afraid you'll have to count me out. I have to be up early tomorrow for school. I want to prepare some papers for the girls.'

'Oh.' That deflated the other girl for precisely one second, then she turned her girlish charm to David, and said pleadingly, 'And what about you? Don't tell me that you have to be up early as well!' She somehow managed to make that sound like the most unutterably dull thing anyone in the world cold choose to do.

Dominic was standing a little apart, observing this cabaret with a hint of impatience.

'Stop forcing yourself on to these people,' he said, folding his arms. 'Remember what I said about making a fool of yourself?'

'Am I making a fool of myself?' She looked at David, who shook his head in a dazed manner, then she turned triumphantly to Dominic and said, 'There! Does that mean you'll come with me for a night-cap somewhere?' she persisted hopefully, while Dominic's face began to darken with irritation.

'I really can't,' David said apologetically.

'Have to be up early?'

'No!' he denied a little too quickly, which made Katherine suddenly want to burst out laughing.

'Come along.' Dominic began dragging the girl along to his car.

She said loudly, over her shoulder, 'Why not, then?'

'I have to drop Katherine back home, for one!' he called back, and Katherine ground her teeth together in frustration. Why on earth did he have to drag her name into it as his excuse?

'These people,' Dominic said, grinding to a halt and looking at his companion as if he wanted to throttle her, 'probably want to spend the night together. They do not want you breaking up their evening.'

'Oh,' said Jack, as if that thought hadn't seriously crossed her mind at all. She looked at both of them and asked candidly, 'Do you?'

'Do we, what?' David asked.

'Want to spend the night together?'

There was a heavy silence and Katherine groaned inwardly to herself. She could feel Dominic's eyes boring through her and she remained silent. Let David talk his way out of this one, she decided.

'Oh,' he said after a while, rising to the occasion by saying the one thing she least needed him to say. 'Katherine and I are just friends.' He gave her arm a little squeeze and she looked at him with utter frost in her eyes.

She realised that she had wanted Dominic to believe that she and David were an item; she wanted him to believe that there was someone, something, in her life, that things had moved on for her too.

'I'm sure Dominic doesn't want you gallivanting all over town with a strange man,' she said. I sound as though I'm telling off a child, she thought, although the other girl didn't appear to mind in the slightest.

'Dominic will be fine without me around for a couple of hours,' she said airily, not in the least perturbed by the hard, angry lines of his face. 'Won't you?' She looked at him with a broad grin. 'Dear friend?' Then she spun back to Katherine. 'He can drop you back to your house, in fact. You two can chat about Claire and the importance of early nights.' She slipped her arm into David's and said brightly, 'Where's your car?'

'Over there.' He pointed to his battered second-hand excuse for an automobile, and then looked rather ruefully at Dominic's sleek BMW. 'Not much by way of transport compared to this.'

'It has character,' Jack informed him, and they were both laughing as they walked towards it.

Katherine stood precisely where she was until David had

started his car, then she turned to Dominic and said awkwardly, 'I apologise about this.'

'Jack can persuade most people to do most things she wants them to,' he said grimly, opening the passenger door for her and then slamming it.

The car had an expensive feel, with that unmistakable aroma of leather. Katherine rested her head back and felt her body tense as he slipped into the driver's seat and started the engine.

Did he not mind that his girlfriend was ready to leave him behind in favour of the bright lights? she wondered, and then she decided that he probably liked that, liked bold, adventurous women who laughed a lot, dressed in seductive clothes and were drawn to nightspots like moths to a candle. It was, after all, what he had liked about her all those years ago, wasn't it?

'Where do you live?' he asked, half turning to her, and she muttered her address, giving him directions to her house.

They didn't talk about Jack and she stole sidelong glances at the tight set of his face.

He had always struck her as the sort of man who needed a challenge in a woman. He had always been highly delighted at her own forthrightness, and she had blossomed under those amused, sexy eyes. She had said things without her usual careful consideration, had voiced opinions with a sharp wit that had made him laugh. Maybe he liked the fact that his girlfriend was quite happy to defy him and do her own thing, weather he approved or not.

The car pulled up outside the house and he switched off the engine, which she thought unnecessary, but she didn't comment on that.

She yanked down the handle of the door and said with a nervous laugh, 'Thank you for driving me back and I do apologise again for David leaving you with no option. He's normally such a sensible person, I can't quite imagine what's got into him.'

He didn't make the dismissive noises which she had expected. Instead he turned to her and said in a hard voice, 'What was he like?'

Katherine shot him a puzzled look. 'Who?' she asked.

'Don't patronise me, Katherine,' he hissed. 'You know who I'm talking about.'

They stared at each other until she could feel the blood draining away from her face, and she turned away, hurriedly and clumsily trying to open the car door.

'You haven't answered me.' His hand snaked out and twisted her around to face him.

'Does it matter? It's all in the past.'

'I'll decide what matters or not. Six years ago you walked out on me and, as far as I am concerned, there are still a few loose ends to be tied up.'

'And if I refuse to oblige?'

'You won't,' Dominic said harshly.

The street-lamp outside her house, very reassuring on those winter nights when she arrived back at her house after dark, threw his angular face into half-shadow and gave him an alarming, devilish look.

'I don't intend to be cross-examined by you,' she said in her firmest voice, the one which she pulled out whenever one of the girls in her class showed signs of getting a little out of hand. 'I'm going inside now and I want you to leave me alone. Just because your girlfriend's behaviour has put you in a foul temper it doesn't mean that I have to sit here and suffer for that. Haven't you got a punch-bag at your house? Or a dart-board? Or some other inanimate object you could take out your frustrations on?'

It was a good speech. Cool, precise, with no indication

of the nervous confusion raging inside her. When she had known him before, he had never seen that cool, precise side to her. It should, she decided, throw him off-course.

She pulled her arm away from him, opened the car door and hurried out to the house.

She was fumbling in her bag for her key when she realised that he was standing next to her, or rather looming over her, darkly menacing, and she spun round to face him with somewhat less of her self-composure.

'What do you think you're doing?' Her voice was high and disconcerted.

'Waiting for you to open the front door.'

'I can see myself in, thank you,' she informed him, pushing open the door, and he didn't answer. He just reached out, pushed back the door and stepped inside.

Then he switched on the light by the door and proceeded to look around him coolly, calmly and unhurriedly, while Katherine fumed impotently on the sidelines.

She had decorated the small place as prettily as she could on a limited budget and working around quite a few inherited bits of furniture, some of them rather too heavy for the room, but which, for reasons which she could not explain, she had felt compelled to keep.

The décor was mostly green, a safe colour, she knew, and the only flashes of startling colour were on the walls—pictures which she had picked up from various junk shops over the years, a few Mexican plates which evoked the odd aroma of foreign shores, and lots of flowers from the garden. Pink, yellow, white, red—great bunches of them heaped into vases.

'Happy?' she asked in a tight, angry voice. 'Satisfied now that you've forced your way into my home?'

'Never satisfied,' he said smoothly, turning to face her

with his hands in his pockets, 'until you tell me about the man you left me for.'

'Then you'll have to lead a life of discontent, because I don't intend to do anything of the sort.' She deposited her bag on the coffee-table in front of the sofa and then sat down on one of the upright chairs and stared at him with antagonism. 'Why does it matter, anyway?' she asked angrily. 'Why does something that happened six years ago matter?'

One minute he was lounging in the centre of the room, dwarfing it, the next minute he was bending over her, his hands on either side of the chair, and his face was a mask of dark fury.

'Because,' he grated, 'no one has ever walked out on me before. Because I can usually read people. Because what I read in you didn't add up to what you did.'

His face, only inches away from her own, sent shivers of panic through her, but she said coldly enough, 'Oh, so what we have here is a massive case of wounded pride, is it?'

'I can only suppose that this man was someone utterly undesirable,' he ground out, and she flinched back. 'Was he, dammit?'

She didn't answer; there was no answer. There was no man. But she could never tell him the truth because that would have been even more damaging than the lie.

'Is that why you're running behind this David character?' he asked. 'Demeaning yourself in the process?' He gave a bark of cruel laughter and straightened up. 'I saw the way you looked at him when he admitted that there was nothing going on between the two of you.' He began prowling through the room, like a tiger in a cage, and just as dangerous. 'You were furious. It must be galling to have spent four years throwing yourself at a man who's not interested. And what a man! Tame, unexciting.'

'You don't know him!' she snapped defensively, and he turned round to stare at her with a witheringly cold look in his eyes.

'You'd eat him alive,' he said, followed by something in very rapid French which she didn't begin to understand. 'It would be like pairing up chalk and cheese and expecting a happy outcome.' He laughed again, and there was the same sharp, cruel edge to his laughter that had been there before, which made the blood rush to her head.

'And what about you?' she asked heatedly.

No one, she thought, could rouse her the way this man could. She was normally such a placid person. How could she change into this fiery creature when in his presence? She looked at him with deep loathing.

'What about me?'

'You and that young girl! Someone prepared to have a night out with a perfect stranger! Do you think that you're really qualified to make sweeping observations on other people's relationships when your own is so odd?' She took a deep breath and carried on in a rush. 'It's OK for you to have a free and open relationship, is it? But wrong for other people?' She laughed angrily. 'You must really love her to let her do precisely as she likes.'

'Oh, yes,' he said softly, coming close to her, standing over her. 'I love her a great deal. She's my sister.'

CHAPTER FOUR

'OF COURSE I'm his sister.' Jacqueline Duvall drained the last remnant of her frothy coffee with every indication of enjoyment.

It was Saturday morning and she had come over to apologise, she said, for her behaviour a few evenings ago. Katherine had answered the door to her and her surprise at seeing the girl on her doorstep had been so evident that Jack had burst out laughing, a high, merry laugh that lit her face up and showed how young she really was.

'Why didn't he say so from the beginning?' Katherine asked, pouring them both another cup and spooning the frothy cream on top. She sat down and looked at the other girl, and realised that, now that she knew, she could see the similarities between Dominic and his sister. Both were dark, both striking in their different ways, except that whereas Dominic's good looks were hard and vaguely forbidding, his sister's were fresh and open.

'I have no idea.' Jack shrugged. 'This coffee is delicious. I could keep drinking it forever. I'm mad about coffee, addicted to it.' She paused and then reverted to the subject of her brother as though she hadn't digressed. 'Dominic is strange sometimes. Not easy to fathom. I really do not know why he didn't tell you from the beginning that he and I were brother and sister. Perhaps he wanted to make sure that you didn't—how do I say it?—take a fancy to him.'

She said that without any overtones of malice. Just a statement of fact.

'Why should I take a fancy to your brother?' Katherine asked politely, but it was an effort to drag the corresponding smile to her lips.

Jacqueline obviously didn't know a thing about their briefly shared past. She would only have been a teenager at the time, living in another country, wrapped up in parties and boys.

The other girl looked at her with vast amusement and Katherine immediately felt obliged to say in starchy self-defence that not every woman was automatically interested in a man simply because he happened to be passable-looking.

'He's immensely rich too,' Jack pointed out, arching her eyebrows.

'Money and good looks aren't necessarily going to turn every woman's head.'

'You must be the exception!' She laughed gaily. 'He has women falling over him.'

'Perhaps some of them are short-sighted,' Katherine mused, grinning at the thought that that conjured up.

'Not so you would notice! Anyway,' she continued artlessly, 'Dominic has had his fingers burnt once with a woman. He's very careful now.'

Katherine's heart speeded up. Was she referring to her? Had Dominic perhaps mentioned her without naming names? She tried to stifle the thrill that gave her.

'What woman was that?' she asked casually, sipping some of her coffee.

'His wife, of course. An awful woman.' The beautifully shaped mouth turned down with remembered distaste. 'She married him because she was in love with the idea of being married to Dominic Duvall. All the cachet that that en-

tailed! The important friends, the pictures in the newspaper
at regular intervals. When Dominic couldn't stand it any
longer and said that he wanted a divorce, Françoise did the
one thing to hurt him most. She took Claire away. Changed
her name to Laudette. Tried to prevent him from seeing her
as much as she could.' The girl shuddered. 'Then the accident. It is good that he has Claire now, but he is a bitter
man.' She stood up and gathered her khaki-coloured knap-
sack from the chair. 'You are a nice woman. Don't make
the mistake of falling for him. You would live to regret it.
Yes, I am sure,' she said thoughtfully, 'that Dominic was
warning you off by letting you think that I was not his
sister.' She shrugged her shoulders elegantly. 'But you're
far too sensible, anyway, aren't you? David says that you're
unflappable.'

'Oh, yes.' The forced smile was back on her lips. 'Very
sensible. Highly unflappable.' Bed at nine every night, flat
shoes, open fire and a good book during winter, gardening
in summer. What an exciting person I am.

'I would like very much to see him again,' Jack said
hesitantly. 'He says that you and he are not...'

'No, we aren't...' Katherine smiled, feeling old in the
face of this youthful enthusiasm. 'You needn't ask my per-
mission,' she said, and Jack smiled back with relief.

'Please, don't tell Dominic about David,' she said on her
way out, as an afterthought. 'He can be a little over-
protective about me. He thinks that men are only interested
in me for one thing. My inheritance. I have stopped arguing
the point with him.'

'It'll be our little secret,' Katherine said obligingly, walking out of the house with the girl and standing at the bottom
of the path to wave her off.

The minute she was back in the house, she gave full rein
to the anger that had been simmering away inside her.

So he had wanted to warn her off him, had he? He had wanted to make it clear from the very start that she shouldn't entertain any misplaced ideas about rekindling what they had had, had he? Perhaps he had imagined that an ageing woman, on the shelf, as she undoubtedly was, might get it into her head that a six-month fling, six years ago, was reason enough to think herself still desirable.

She did the housework with venom, and then, on the spur of the moment, she jumped into her car and headed off to his house on the outskirts of the town. She knew where he lived from Claire: it had been one of those snippets of information which had slipped out in conversation. She had no need of the address because she knew the house by name alone. Everyone in the town would. It was one of those houses, of which there were only a handful, which had a history all of its own.

She had no idea whether he would be there or not, and she didn't care whether he would want to see her or not. She just wanted to get one thing straight with him, and that was that she was not some kind of laughable threat to him.

It irked her that he had felt the need to warn her off, in however subtle a manner. Didn't he think that his manifest dislike for her would be enough? Did he imagine that she was so thick-skinned and so desperate that she would pursue him now as the lost chance which she could recapture?

The house was a huge Victorian mansion set back from the road and hidden by trees. The drive swept down to the house, past a small cottage which, rumour had it, had once housed a mad relative of the landowner several decades before, and past a block of stables, now disused.

Katherine drove past the cottage and past the stables as quickly as she could comfortably go on the gravel, and stopped the car next to the BMW, which was carelessly parked at an angle in the courtyard.

She was hardly thinking straight at all. She knew that Jack had meant no harm in warning her off her brother, just as she had meant no harm in explaining why he was wary of women. Jacqueline Duvall was one of those people who generously believed that the truth couldn't possibly hurt.

She slammed the car door behind her, glared at it as it stood there, small, apologetic, in need of a wash, and then stormed towards the front door.

It was almost a shame that there was no doorknocker, but there wasn't. It was a bell, one of those old-fashioned ones which she could hear ringing through the house from outside and, after she had fumed on the doorstep for half a minute, the front door was opened by a middle-aged woman who looked at her curiously and seemed about to say that they weren't interested in buying anything.

Something in Katherine's face must have made her realise, though, that the slim woman in the brown dress and sandals was not interested in selling anything.

She said a little dubiously, and without fully opening the door, 'Yes?'

'Mr Duvall. Is he in?'

'Yes.'

'In that case, may I see him?'

'Who is it, may I ask?' the woman asked suspiciously. She spoke in broken English, and Katherine realised that this housekeeper had probably come from France with him. Had probably known him for years. Was that why she was so suspicious? Did she have a lot of experience of unwanted women showing up on the doorstep and demanding to see the master of the house? That made her fume a little more.

'Miss Lewis,' Katherine said clearly. 'Claire's teacher.'

'Ah.' The brow uncreased and she opened the door to

let her enter. 'Monsieur Duvall, he is in the office, working.' She shook her head as though she had some very
distinct thoughts on that but wasn't about to voice them to
a stranger. 'Claire, she is not here. She is out.'

She led the way out of the great hall, with its heavy, dark
banister which swung upstairs, and the myriad doors leading to various rooms, all shut.

Katherine looked around her, feeling slightly dwarfed by
the high ceilings and the immense proportions. It was
smaller than a stately home, but still large enough, she was
sure, to get completely lost in.

The elderly woman was walking ahead, muttering under
her breath in indistinct French, through a large, sunny
room, decorated in shades of yellow, through what appeared to be another small hall, which clearly led out to
the side of the house, and down two steps into a kitchen,
which had been fitted with every modern convenience
known to mankind and in the middle of which was an impressive bottle-green Aga.

Very domestic, Katherine thought, not prepared to be
anything but acid. Not that the lord and master probably
knows how to knock up anything more complicated than a
boiled egg.

There were two other rooms, tiled in a dark red stone,
in which there were cupboards, two fridges, a freezer and
enough storage space, she thought, to house the entire contents of her modest dwelling. Then the woman knocked on
a door, which looked as though it should have led to the
courtyard—simply because it was hard to believe that the
house actually continued. But it didn't.

It led, down one step, to the plushest room Katherine had
ever seen.

It was exactly like an office, but with all the expensive
trappings of a home. The carpet was white, as were the

walls, which were beamed at the top, and there were small paintings by the far doorway, through which she could see more stairs. Did the house never end? she wondered.

She almost forgot to be angry. In fact, she was so taken aback by the grandeur of the place that she had almost forgotten why she had come in the first place.

She remembered soon enough, when Dominic appeared in the doorway and stood there, staring at her, expensively casual in a short-sleeved cream shirt and a pair of dirt-green trousers.

'Well, well, well,' he drawled. 'What a surprise.' He looked neither surprised nor particularly pleased to see her, and she stuck her chin out defiantly, feeling more like a teenager than a grown woman.

'I want to have a word with you, Dominic Duvall,' she said, with her hands on her hips.

He replied smoothly, looking behind her, 'That will be all, Lise.' The door closed quietly behind them, and he said calmly, 'I dislike scenes in front of Lise.'

'How noble,' Katherine retorted. 'And is she used to that sort of thing happening? Women barging in to create scenes with you?'

'Ah, so we've established that you've barged your way into my house to create a scene.' He spun round on his heels and headed up the stairs, and she had no option but to follow him.

The staircase, unlike the grand affair in the main hall, was tiny and narrow.

This part of the house was clearly pre-Victorian. The upstairs room, which housed a large desk of stripped pine, a computer terminal, two telephones and a fax machine, was heavily beamed and quite small.

He perched on the edge of the desk, folded his arms and looked at her with mild interest.

'I take it that you haven't beaten a path to my house to tell me something about Claire's progress at school?'

'That's right.' She walked towards him with her arms folded. 'I've come here to tell you, Mr Duvall, that you are way out of line if you think that you need to warn me off you. You may go through life imagining that you're irresistible to every member of the opposite sex, but when it comes to me you're about as irresistible as a bowl of congealed porridge.'

'Since when?' He raised his eyebrows with something which looked insultingly like amusement, and she could have slapped him.

'Since now,' she told him, 'which is all that counts.' She hoped that she was being meaningful enough, because the one thing that infuriated her even more than him thinking that he needed to warn her off was him thinking that she still hankered after him.

'And why,' he asked, 'have you suddenly decided to climb into your car and storm round here to tell me that you're not interested in me?'

Katherine glared, and hoped that he wasn't thinking along the lines of the lady who doth protest too much.

'I had a visit,' she said, 'from your sister.'

'Ah.' His face relaxed into a crooked smile.

'You could have told me that she was your sister when we met. There was no need to pretend that she wasn't. Did you think that I might leap at you because, at the age of thirty-one, I might feel that I'm gathering cobwebs?'

She hadn't quite meant to say that and, now that she had, she realised awkwardly that it put her at a disadvantage.

'And do you?' he asked softly, lazily. 'Why,' he continued, changing the subject and at the same time managing to convey that he would get back to it just as soon as it suited him, 'don't I get Lise to bring up some coffee? Or would you prefer tea?'

'This was not meant to be a social call.'

'Which is hardly any reason to refuse a cup of coffee.'

'I'll have tea,' she said, slightly deflated and somehow blaming him for this state of affairs.

She could deal with him when she was in control, the teacher at the front of the class, or else when she was furious, because fury left little room for thought. It was much harder to deal with him when she was on the receiving end of his formidable self-control, or, worse, that crooked smile that could charm the birds from the trees. That made her feel girlish, and girlishness was something that confused her because it wasn't a part of her life.

Again, without warning, she had the oddest sensation of wanting more than she had, of glimpsing a star when she had come to believe that there were none. It was a stirring deep inside her that shifted everything just a little out of focus.

He vanished out of the room, leaving her to her thoughts which, as far as she was concerned, were very unwelcome companions indeed, and reappeared fifteen minutes later with a tray.

'She hates these stairs,' he said, shifting aside a wad of papers to make room for the tray. 'She says they're too steep but, frankly, I think it's a sign of Lise getting older.' He poured them both some tea, then said, resuming his position against the desk and indicating a chair to her, 'Now, where were we?'

Katherine sat down. 'We weren't anywhere,' she said. 'I had made my point and was on my way out, and you then insisted that I had some tea.'

'You were about to tell me whether you feel as though you are gathering cobwebs.'

'I was not about to do any such thing.'

'Thirty-one, a schoolteacher, out here in the provinces. Do you think that your life is closing in?'

'Still a young woman, doing a job that I love, surrounded by beautiful countryside. Why should I?'

He laughed, his green eyes glittering.

'I don't live here against my will,' Katherine said quietly. 'Nor do I teach through necessity. I like it.'

'Yet you pursue a man like the one who took my sister out. Why? Where does the attraction lie?'

She went pink. 'David is a good man.' She rested the teacup and saucer on her lap and thought, Why should I let him feel that there has been no one for the past six years? Why give him the satisfaction? 'He's steady, he's reliable.'

'Not the most exciting qualities in the world.'

'I don't crave excitement,' she said quickly. 'I did once, but...'

'You mean in London?' His voice was sharp and demanding, and it made her realise how guarded she had to be in her responses to him.

'Yes.' She nodded. 'Now I have to go.' She began walking towards the doorway. There was no door there, simply an arch.

'But now all that is behind you?' he asked softly, from behind her. 'Is that why you cultivate this dowdy image?' She felt him reach out, and then he pulled the elastic band from her plait and spread his fingers in her hair.

The feel of his hand coiled in her long hair was like a vast electric charge going through her. He pulled the strands of the plait until her hair fell down her back, then he turned her round to face him. His fingers tangled in the mass of her hair made it impossible for her to run.

'That's better,' he said with satisfaction, and he gave her a long, cool look that was appraising rather than sexual.

'Give me back,' she muttered, her cheeks hectic with colour, 'that elastic band.'

'Is that the tone you use on those little girls when they start misbehaving?'

She ignored that. 'Now.'

'My blood is curdling with fright,' he drawled, 'but no, I don't think I will return it to you. You look far nicer with your hair loose. More like that wild, carefree nymph I used to know.'

'I am neither wild nor carefree,' she heard herself say stiffly, and in her voice she could hear the unsteady promise of tears, which she bit back.

'Perhaps David would be more attracted to you if you unbent a little.'

'Don't give me advice on my private life.'

The abundance of dark hair falling around her was embarrassing. Why on earth had she never had it cut? It was as if that gay, light-hearted creature who had fallen head over heels in love with Dominic Duvall all those years ago had been locked away in a room. All that was left of her was this hair, spilling down like silk. To have had it chopped off would have been like locking the door of the room. Had she subconsciously veered away from doing that?

The question ran through her head, puzzling her, frightening her, because, when she had thought that everything was sorted out, that she was in control of her life, they made her think that perhaps she wasn't after all.

'Perhaps he wouldn't be so eager to pursue my sister,' Dominic said smoothly.

'He isn't. He took your sister out once because he was forced into it, but that was all.' She spoke quickly, spontaneously defending Jack, remembering what the girl had said about her brother's over-protectiveness.

As soon as she had spoken, though, she wondered why on earth she had bothered. She didn't want to involve herself in this family. Let them get on with their own internal problems. The best thing she could do would be to steer clear of them.

Dominic looked at her through narrowed, speculative eyes.

'He didn't strike me as a man under pressure.'

'He's too polite to kick up a fuss over something like that,' she muttered under her breath.

'Is that what you tell yourself? And what will you tell yourself the next time temptation gets in his way? That he's just too polite to refuse?'

Katherine swung round and began walking away.

'I'm not finished with you,' he said from behind her, and she hesitated just a fraction too long. Instead of running swiftly down the stairs, she paused, with her back to him.

'You force your way into this house on some strange mission to defend yourself, but it's quite pointless. You're no more interested in me than I am in you, and I'm fully aware of that. I have no idea what my sister said to you, but I don't see the necessity of warning you off me. Why should I? I made a mistake with you once and I'm not a man to make the same mistake a second time.'

'Good.' She turned to face him.

She had swept her hair over one shoulder and she twirled the bottom of the mane in her fingers.

'But if you're so concerned about your precious pride, then why don't you look at your behaviour with this man of yours? Four years of chasing, and for what? You tell me that your life is perfect, but I look at you and I can only think that desperation is driving you on to accept a man like that, who clearly doesn't want any more from you than the occasional meal out and a friendly ear.'

He had taken a few steps towards her and she stared at him angrily, her heart thudding.

'Oh, you know all this after a five-minute meeting, do you? How clever! But you're hardly in a fit position to lecture about relationships, are you? Jack told me about...' Here her voice fizzled out. She saw a flash of fury cross his face.

'Told you about...what?'

'Nothing.'

'Told you about my wife, I take it?'

'I'm sorry,' Katherine mumbled. 'I had no right to mention your wife.'

'No.' Dominic's voice was cold. 'You hadn't. But now that you have, you might just as well hear it from my mouth. My marriage to Françoise was a mistake. In fact, the only good thing to emerge from it was Claire. Françoise was demanding, avaricious, vain.'

'Why did you marry her in the first place?'

'Because,' he said grimly, 'she was exciting.' His lips twisted into a sneer. 'And excitement is an addictive drug, isn't it? Unfortunately, it is rarely enough to take two people through a marriage.'

'Does excitement mean that much to you?' she asked faintly.

'What are the alternatives? Tedium? Monotony? The relentless treadmill of boredom?'

'Of course not.'

'Of course not,' he drawled in a vaguely sneering voice. 'And you would know, would you? You tell me that I'm unfit to lecture about relationships, but I hardly see how you're in a position to lecture about the nuts and bolts of marriage.'

'I wasn't lecturing,' Katherine protested heatedly. She

had dropped her hands to her sides and her fists were clenched.

'Have you had any excitement in your life since London?' he asked softly, and now he was standing so close to her that she could feel his restless energy radiating out from him in waves. It was an unsettling feeling. She felt like someone standing on a mountain, where the air was thin and breathing was difficult.

'Excitement isn't only about clubs and expensive dinners out and foreign travel,' she muttered defensively.

'So tell me what it is about. I'm dying to hear.'

'No, you're not,' she said, taking a deep breath and staring him straight in the eyes. 'You're dying to make fun of me, of what I do now. I know that I'm not the same person you met in London six years ago, Dominic Duvall. I know that my life probably seems utterly dull to someone like you but, believe it or not, it's the life I love.'

'How did you get involved in teaching?' he asked curiously, and his eyes were sharp and searching. 'Did David persuade you into it?'

'No one could persuade me into a career I didn't want. You must think that I have no mind of my own.'

'Women can be very gullible when they're in love.'

She didn't know how this conversation had arrived where it had, but alarm was slowly replacing tension. All these questions, softly spoken but insistent nevertheless, were targeted, she suspected, at discovering why, precisely why, she had walked out on him.

The past was never over. It allowed itself to be shut away for the sake of convenience, but circumstance could easily pull it out once again.

Was this what had happened? Had he forgotten all about her, only to find that, now their paths had crossed, he needed to make sense of what must have been nonsensical at the time?

He wasn't interested in her. He himself admitted it. He was a man who enjoyed excitement. He needed it. In his professional life as well as his personal life. He had married his wife because she gave him that thrill of excitement, and even though that had failed he would always be drawn to the same sort of woman. He had only ever gone out with her because, at that time in her own life, when she was living on a razor's edge and fuelled with the kind of raw energy which she would never again want to recapture, she had appealed to him.

'Gullible women,' she said calmly, 'are gullible all the time, whether they're in love or not. I am not a gullible woman.'

'You make that sound like a virtue,' he said with mild contempt, 'but there's no virtue to living life on one level all the time. Does David turn you on?' He asked the question as naturally as though he was asking the time of day.

'You must be joking if you think that I'm going to answer that.'

Her eyes were wide and startled. She backed a little and came up against the banister.

'Why shouldn't you? The only reason you wouldn't would be if you were scared to, and the only reason you'd be scared to would be if the answer was no.'

He laughed under his breath, as though he found the situation amusing, and then reached out his arms and propped them on either side of her.

'Of course, I know the answer to the question already,' he told her lazily. 'He doesn't turn you on in the slightest. It's very easy to pick up signals from other people's body language. They often give themselves away without having to speak at all. Poor David. He might appeal to you as a possible marriage partner, in the absence of anyone else, but sexually he doesn't appeal at all, does he?'

'Why ask me? You already know all the answers, or so you claim.'

'Has there been anyone in your life in the past six years, Katherine? You had your fling with me and then ran back to the man you wanted. But that didn't work out. Did you make the decision then to bury yourself in your job and make believe that you were happy?'

He was still bitter. Under all that cool self-control, under all that cynical amusement, he was still bitter. It made no difference that he no longer wanted her and certainly felt nothing for her, the bitterness was still there, running through him like a black thread.

She saw that in a blinding flash of comprehension.

'Stop trying to pigeon-hole me,' she said angrily. 'You'd like nothing better, I know, than for me to break down and confess that my life was one long tale of misery and woe, but I'm not about to do that! You have no idea what fulfilment I get from teaching children, from watching them grow, from sowing seeds of curiosity in their minds. You may well amuse yourself by thinking that it's all second-best, but you'd be wrong.'

'But there's more to life than sowing seeds in children's minds, isn't there? When night falls and there are no children around, how do you console yourself?'

'I might ask you the same question. When you walk out of your office and take off your cloak of all-powerful tycoon, how do you console yourself?'

She was amazed that she could argue back at him so coherently. It was as if words and emotions were working together, gathering momentum, making her say things that she would otherwise have kept to herself if she had thought about it. She was so used to keeping things to herself, but something about this man made her want to open herself up and fling the contents of her mind at him.

Mulishness, anger, stubborn pride, she supposed. All those negative things which had not been a part of her life for a very long time.

'I've had women,' he shrugged, and didn't take his eyes off her face. She felt like a specimen under observation.

'How rewarding for you,' she said, her voice laced with sarcasm, and she was gratified to see his mouth tighten at her tone.

'Isn't it? More rewarding than feeling as though commitment is necessary, regardless of to whom that commitment is given, I would say.'

He was referring to David again, and she looked at him icily, until he began to laugh, standing back and folding his arms across his chest.

'What a look!' he said. 'Have I offended you?'

Her back was beginning to ache from the pressure of pushing herself as far back against the banister as she could, and she shifted slightly.

'Of course not.' She flung him a stiff look which made him laugh a little harder. 'I'm just so glad that I could be of some amusement to the lord of the manor.'

At which she began walking down the stairs, aware that he was behind her, still laughing under his breath.

They reached the kitchen door just as Jack was pulling up in her Jeep, screeching to a halt and releasing her five-year-old passenger.

'You forgot something,' he said, bending down to whisper into her ear, and she turned to him sharply.

'What?'

'Your precious little elastic band for your hair.' He held it up between two fingers, and she gave him a look that would have wilted a flower in full bloom, but which only made his lips begin to twitch again.

'Thank you.' Her voice was cold. He might find it highly humorous to laugh at her, but she wasn't about to share in his amusement. She whipped her hair back into a makeshift ponytail, and when she turned round Claire was standing in front of her, delighted at the unexpected presence of her schoolteacher.

Had she come to see her? she asked joyfully. Jack was approaching them more slowly, her eyes flitting from her brother to Katherine.

'Please come in,' Claire pleaded, 'for a glass of orange squash.'

'Miss Lewis probably doesn't care for orange squash, Claire,' her father said.

'Ribena, then?'

'Perhaps another day,' Katherine said gently, smiling at Jack, who was trying to ask questions with her eyes and failing. She walked out into the sunshine towards her car, holding Claire's hand and listening to the childish chatter, while Dominic went ahead to open her door for her with a theatrically mocking flourish. That delighted Claire, but only annoyed Katherine still further.

'I'm sure Miss Lewis will come back another day,' he said soothingly to his daughter, picking her up, and Katherine could tell from the way he did that that it was not an everyday occurrence. The child looked simultaneously flattered and bemused.

'Of course I will,' she agreed, while the expression on her face told Dominic in no uncertain terms that the possibility of that was as remote as the possibility of her taking a trip to the moon for her next holiday.

'Of course you will,' he said with a hint of mockery.

'After all, you enjoyed your little visit here today so much, didn't you?' He raised his eyebrows and, after a brief wave to Claire, Katherine started up the car and swung it out of the long drive. She didn't look back.

CHAPTER FIVE

BY THE time half-term drew round, the days were getting shorter and there was that feel in the air of cold times ahead.

Katherine loved autumn and winter. She loved the changing colours of the leaves from green to yellow to deep red, and she loved the dramatic, stark landscape of winter. She loved the early evenings, when it was acceptable to get back to her little house and spend all evening with the curtains drawn, listening to the wind and reading a good book.

There was an open fire in the lounge, and despite advice from her friends that it would be far simpler to replace it with a gas one, she resolutely refused. She enjoyed the glow of the flames; she enjoyed the energy expended in stacking it with logs.

As October drew to an end, with no more school for a week while the children enjoyed their half-term, she drove back to her house and tried very hard to recapture that contentment she had always felt at the thought of simply lazing around in a warm house, knowing that outside was cold and dark.

She would start her new book; she would make herself a wonderful pasta meal; she would brew some real coffee afterwards and not the usual instant stuff.

She let herself into the house and said aloud, into the emptiness, that this week off was going to be bliss.

Wasn't this just the thing she had always longed for? she thought to herself. How she had hated the long winter months when she had been younger. Being cooped up in the house, timidly trying to tiptoe round her demanding mother, trying to fade into the background, on the off-chance that her presence might go unnoticed. For years now she had been able to do anything she pleased, and for years she had relished the luxury of her privacy, but for some reason things seemed different now.

She was conscious of a silly feeling of discontent, of suddenly wanting more than just peace and solitude for her week's break.

But—and this frustrated her—what?

She made herself a cup of very sweet tea, tucked herself on the sofa and began jotting down a few rudimentary plans for what she would do with the children when they were back at school.

The slow approach to Christmas was always a busy time. There was the nativity play, a thoroughly amateur event, which the children enthusiastically threw themselves into and which she enjoyed hugely. She had two outings lined up, one to the local fire station, which the children would adore because they would all feel as though they were meeting Fireman Sam in person, no less.

She forced herself to begin sketching the plot for the nativity play, which she always did in conjunction with two of the other teachers.

But her mind was wandering. It had been wandering ever since Dominic Duvall had re-entered her life and, try as she might, she couldn't seem to contain it on a leash.

She lay back and stared at the ceiling and thought again, for the hundredth time, about the last time she had seen him, which was two weeks ago. She had stormed over, intent on putting him straight on a couple of things, intent on making it clear that she felt nothing for him, that there was no need for him to fear that she would become a nuisance, but now, when she sat down and thought about it, she couldn't remember whether she had achieved what she had set out to do or not.

She could only recall the heavy beating of her heart, the leap of her senses whenever he had looked at her, the feel of his fingers when he had reached out and freed her hair.

She closed her eyes with a shaky sigh, and was trying to work out what it all meant when there was a sharp knock on the door.

It was David. She hadn't seen him for quite some time, although he had occasionally called her on the telephone—quick calls that lacked the intimacy of their previous conversations.

'I'm glad you're in,' he said. 'I wasn't sure whether you would be.'

'Where else would I be?' She laughed and walked back into the hall, hearing him quietly shut the door behind him.

'I've just made some tea,' she said over her shoulder. 'Would you like a cup? Or has your unruly class driven you to stronger things?'

'Not yet.' He grinned. 'I put my foot down at those tyrants driving me to drink. Besides—' he followed her into the kitchen and sat down at the table '—I must confess that they haven't been too bad recently. In fact, they actually seem to listen when I talk to them these days.'

'How alarming for you!' Katherine said, laughing at the surprise in his voice at the admission. 'However are you going to cope?'

She poured him some tea, extracted a tin of biscuits from the cupboard, pleasantly surprised to find that there were more there than she had anticipated, and then sat down opposite him.

'Now,' she said, 'tell me why I haven't seen you for such a long time, and why, whenever you call, you sound as though you're about to rush off. Have I developed some awful odour problem?'

He dipped his biscuit in his tea, took a bite with great relish and then informed her, with uncharacteristic bluntness, that he had been seeing a lot of Jack.

'Have you?' Katherine raised her eyebrows in surprise.

'She can be very persistent,' he said, smiling. 'Like a dog with a bone.'

'But how do you feel about being a bone?'

'Quite good, actually.'

'Dogs bite, David,' she said thoughtfully. 'I wouldn't like to see you hurt.' She looked at him evenly. 'I mean, she's a very nice girl, but she comes from a world that's quite different from yours. Or mine, for that matter.' She saw him frown at that, and rushed on. 'You know that I don't mean to be awful when I say that. But I like you, and what's the point in liking someone if you can't be honest with them? I wouldn't like to think that you were being used as some kind of novelty for Jacqueline Duvall.'

She wasn't thinking of Jacqueline Duvall when she said that. She was thinking of Dominic. But weren't they cut from the same mould? Supremely self-confident, good-looking people, who had only ever known a life of wealth. People to whom exploitation could perhaps come more easily than to others.

'I know what you're saying.'

'But you don't agree.'

'I'm in love with her.' He looked at her as he said this, and his expression was more resolute than she had ever seen it. 'I know that we're worlds apart, as you say, but I can't opt for the devil I know. My mind might want to do that, but my heart is telling me something else. Can you understand that?'

'No. Yes. I suppose so. What I mean is, I wouldn't, but then, I can understand why someone else might.'

'Why wouldn't you?' His face expressed interest. 'Why is safety so much more appealing than the unknown?'

Because, she wanted to say, the unknown can cause a great deal of pain, because hearts can never be mended fully, because it's better to be in one piece than broken into a thousand bits with no chance of ever being put together again.

'How does she feel about it?' Katherine asked instead, and she noticed the way his eyes lit up as he began talking about her.

She felt an unfamiliar lurch inside her, a twisting of something sharp. She felt like a beggar, standing on the outside and peering through a window into a room full of tables groaning with food, full of people eating to their hearts' content, and she had to tell herself that she was being ridiculous.

'The thing is,' David said, pausing and looking at her seriously, 'we need your help.'

'My help?'

'We want to go away for the half-term and we would rather that her brother didn't know.'

'Why?' Katherine looked at him candidly. 'You're both over the age of consent. I doubt he would come flying behind you with a shot-gun just because you happened to spend a week together.'

'No,' David said slowly, 'but Jack adores her brother. She knows what he would think if he knew that we were seriously seeing one another. He would think that I was after her money.' He said that as a matter of fact, with no resentment at what it implied. 'I'm a fairly impoverished teacher from a fairly impoverished background, and I'm mad about his sister who has money coming out of her ears. Two and two may not make four in this instance, but it very well could, couldn't it?'

'So what am I supposed to do?' Katherine asked, at a loss.

'Simply not say that we've gone off together. If you happen to see him. If he happens to ask. Kath—' he leaned forward urgently '—I need time for this, time to find out whether it's the right thing or not. We both do. We'll never achieve that if Dominic's breathing down our necks and trying to destroy it all before it's hardly begun.'

'I can see that,' she agreed reluctantly.

Dominic could be ruthless, and if he suspected for one moment that his sister was being exploited for her money he would react immediately and decisively.

'You could always get to know him,' she suggested. 'He'll realise that you're no gold-digger when he gets to know you.'

David's face settled into lines of stubborn refusal, which astonished her because she had never known he could be as adamant as this about anything. He had always been light-hearted, easygoing, inclined to cede rather than fight.

'We need undiluted time without his suspicions about my motives. I dearly love his sister and I feel that this is the only way we can go forward. We both do.'

'He'll find out in due course.'

'The bridge will be crossed when we get to it.' There was something else he wanted to ask. She could see the hesitant question hovering, and she waited. 'We've been friends for a long time,' he started, and she threw him a dry look.

'Why do I suspect that there's another favour in the offing?'

'Quite a small one,' David admitted, going red. 'Perhaps you could imply that you and I are still going out. No, no, no—' he held up his hands to ward off her immediate protests '—just listen. I'm not asking you to lie...'

'Simply to economise with the truth?'

'You could hint, if the situation ever arises, which is unlikely. But it'll give us time to sort ourselves out, to find out whether what we're feeling is real or something induced by circumstance.'

His face was flushed and earnest and she found herself nodding reluctantly.

'But that's absolutely it,' she said firmly. 'I refuse to lie outright. If he asks me directly whether you're seeing his sister, then I shall have to tell him the truth. And I won't be coerced into providing alibis of any kind whatsoever.'

'Of course not!' He looked at her, horrified, and she had to smile.

It all seemed a silly game to her, but then, when love was concerned, what ever made sense? Sense was having your life in order; sense was revelling in the calm predictability of your days. She felt that sharp pull inside her again, and brushed it aside. She had toyed with the senseless passion of love and she would never make the same mistake again.

Besides, what real harm would there be in agreeing to what David wanted?

There was little chance that she would bump into Dominic Duvall again, and if she did it would be in the formal setting of a parent-teacher meeting, when the only subject raised would be his daughter.

She doubted that even he, formidable though he was, would be inclined to initiate an argument on his sister's romantic life in the setting of a school.

Once they had sorted themselves out, David would insist

on telling Dominic everything. She knew David well enough for that. She also knew that he would never pursue anyone for their money.

Katherine was settling down comfortably into her usual routine of shops and coffee with her friends, which usually ended up with discussions about school since, inevitably, most of her close friends were also part of the school community, when, in the middle of the week, in the middle of the afternoon, a telephone call disrupted all that.

She had just finished washing her hair and was about to trek to the shops for some food when the phone rang and, for some reason, she automatically thought that it was going to be David. That her neat little summary of him had been wrong, and he had done something utterly unexpected and needed help.

It wasn't David. It was Dominic. She recognised his voice instantly and, even though she was only speaking to him on the phone, she automatically drew her bathrobe tighter round her and glanced suspiciously around the room, as if expecting him to materialise calmly out of nowhere.

'I'm glad you're in,' he said, with a thorough disregard for any polite preliminaries. 'Jack's not around. Vanished somewhere for a week's break and didn't leave me her address. I don't suppose you know where she went?'

'No.'

She was steeling herself for a debate on the subject, but he dropped it immediately and said instead, 'Never mind. You'll do. Claire's not well. She's got some kind of stomach bug and the child-minder says that she needs to stay at home. Jack isn't here, nor is Lise, and anyway, looking after Claire is not one of her duties. She is too old.'

'And what does that have to do with me?' Katherine asked.

'Well, I'm afraid I have a series of high-level meetings today and I can't stay put to look after a sick child.'

'Go right ahead and criticise,' she said coolly, 'but isn't that what parenting is all about?'

'I have no time to listen to your views on parenting,' Dominic said, his voice clipped, and she could picture him looking at his watch impatiently, 'I've already taken enough time off work to drive back to the child-minder and collect Claire. I need to leave as soon as possible. When can you get here?'

'I have no intention of—'

'Yes, you have,' he said, cutting her short.

'Why me?' Katherine asked, resenting the manner in which she was being taken for granted. Why did everyone simply assume that she would never mind putting herself out on their behalf?

'Because I don't know who else to ask,' he said bluntly. 'I could get one the girls at the office to come over, I suppose, but Claire can be awkward with people she doesn't know.'

Katherine sighed. A little sigh of resignation. 'I'll be over in fifteen minutes,' she said. 'I just need to change first.'

'Thank you, Katherine,' he said, after a short pause. 'I do realise that you have a life to lead, and that this is an unnecessary interruption. I'll see you shortly.'

He hung up, and she raced around, shoving clothes on in a haphazard manner, slinging her jacket over the whole uncoordinated mess, and then climbed into the car.

As happened every time she had even the briefest of contact with him, she found herself operating in overdrive, as though her body had been suddenly injected with a large dose of adrenaline.

She made it to the house in twenty minutes, and found

him virtually waiting on the doorstep for her, dressed in an impeccably cut suit.

How was it, she thought, looking up at him, that he always seemed to reduce her to a state of absolute confusion? She stripped off her jacket and almost felt like apologising for the jeans, the baggy jumper and the sneakers.

'When I was a boy,' he said, looking her up and down without, she decided, a great deal of appreciation, 'I always assumed that teachers dressed as starchily out of work as they did for work. At last, I have been proved wrong.'

'I'm normally a lot tidier than this,' Katherine felt compelled to say defensively, 'but I was in a rush to get here.'

He nodded and said, abruptly looking away, 'Claire's upstairs in her bedroom. Feeling sorry for herself.'

'Children do,' Katherine replied tartly, following him up the stairs as he led the way. 'Though not as much as adults.'

She looked at his lean body, his wide, powerful shoulders. How odd to think that she had once caressed that body intimately, run her hands along the sinewed, muscled length of him. Now he was a stranger, and she felt a sudden pang for things lost. Then she was being shown into Claire's bedroom, where Claire was mournfully propped up against some pillows, watching cartoons on a portable television.

She turned to look at them and her little face broke out into a smile.

'I didn't believe that you would come!' she squealed with delight.

Katherine said wryly, 'Are you quite sure that you're ill? You look very healthy to me.' At which Claire immediately looked mournful once more and launched into a childish description of her symptoms, which appeared to range from a sore throat to a headache in her stomach. And all this said with such gravity that Katherine was hard-pressed not to burst out laughing.

She could sense Dominic watching them from behind her, then she heard him say, 'I'll be back a little later.'

'When a little later?' Katherine asked, twisting round to look at him.

'Some time after six,' he drawled, 'and before eight. Is that good enough?'

'No doubt it will have to be,' she said, turning back to face Claire. 'You've missed your calling, though. You should have worked as a plumber. They can never promise definite times for doing anything, either.'

She heard him laugh under his breath as he left the room, and then, for the next few hours, she had a thoroughly good time with Claire.

Holidays, however carefully she planned them, were invariably lonely times for her. Married friends tended to spend their time together, doing all those domestic things which Katherine vaguely assumed to be richly rewarding and totally exclusive of single friends at loose ends.

It was, she had always thought, a bit unfair that people could feel free to call on her whenever they wanted to, but she always thought very carefully when it came to calling on other people.

At thirty-one, single girlfriends were a bit thin on the ground. She had watched them, over the past six years, move from engagement to marriage to children, while she hovered on the sidelines, knowing that they were entering a whole sphere of life which would never be hers.

Once, she had thought that perhaps she should just make do, just summon up the energy to encourage one of the blind dates which her friends would arrange, convinced that they were doing her a good turn.

But she never could. At first, it had been because the spectre of Dominic had still been too close to her heart, and then she had come to accept her solitude, so that the thought of sharing it with someone simply for the sake of having a partner made no sense. By which time it was fairly theoretical anyway, since the blind dates had dried up.

She looked at Claire, who was attempting to build an intricate monster out of some Lego bricks, while grumbling under her breath about the unfairness of being starved of food when her tummy felt much better, and saw Dominic. She saw him from across the great gulf of unspoken truths and wished with passion that he had never returned. She had learned to cope with the spectre, but she couldn't cope with him. It hardly made it any easier to know that the past had made her loathsome for him.

At seven, she told Claire that it was time for bed and got the expected response that she wasn't sleepy.

'I'll read you a story,' Katherine suggested temptingly. 'You can choose the book yourself.'

She looked at the small figure in the nightie fondly, and wondered what it must be like to have a child. Not to be caretaker for dozens of children, whose faces changed from year to year, but to have a child of her own. She had never felt as discontented with her lot as she had done recently, and she wearily realised that it all had to do with Dominic's reappearance, raising questions which unfortunately had no answers, offering a view of things which, inevitably, were unattainable.

Bitterness, she knew, was a pill that left a sour aftertaste for the rest of your life.

His bitterness was as tangible as a wall of steel. But bitterness was not the only wall that lay between them, high and cold and immovable.

There was herself, dull, staid, no longer a Cinderella at the ball—just an ordinary, unexciting woman with nothing to offer a man like Dominic Duvall.

She couldn't even work out what she felt for him any

longer. It wasn't indifference, but it wasn't love either. Love didn't make you jumpy and nervous. Once, she had been wildly passionate about him, but she had also been blissfully serene in his presence, not constantly trying to fight down panic attacks.

She began telling a story to Claire, making it up as she went along. She was good at story-telling. At school, she sometimes played a game of invention with the children. She would start a story, then call on one of them to add a bit, working her way around the class until they arrived at a conclusion.

Every so often, now, she asked Claire to contribute a bit, and after a while she realised that the child had fallen asleep, her arms and legs spread across the bed with child-ish abandon, her mouth half-open.

She went downstairs, and was making herself a cup of coffee when she heard the sound of wheels on the gravel and then the key in the lock of the side door by the kitchen.

'How is Claire?' was the first thing Dominic asked as he walked into the kitchen.

Wasn't it funny, she thought, how his presence could permeate the atmosphere and alter it? She could never talk to him the way she talked to other people—sensibly, calmly, rationally. She always planned to, but somewhere along the way, between her brain relaying the message and the words coming out, something happened and she re-verted to a level of emotional incoherence which was nor-mally alien to her.

'Good,' she now said, looking at him, and even from the opposite end of the table having to ward off that disturbing dynamism he radiated. 'I'm not terribly popular at the mo-ment, though,' she continued, sipping the hot coffee and trying hard to sound casual and adult, and like the school-teacher that she was. 'I've only allowed her a piece of toast for her supper and a little diluted apple juice. I don't think she minded the toast, but she was most put out when I told her that there was no pudding. It took fifteen minutes of persuasion and I had to resort to a biological explanation of the stomach. She only gave in because she got bored with my monologue.'

Dominic looked amused at that. 'So, she should be well enough to go to her child-minder in the morning.' It was more a statement than a question.

'She should be, yes,' Katherine said, 'but it would be nice for her if you could take the day off, or maybe half a day.'

'What for?'

'It would cheer her up.'

'I can't afford the time off,' he said flatly, and he turned away from her to pour himself some coffee.

'You own the company,' she pointed out to his back, thinking that he could at least have the decency to look at her when she was talking. 'Surely you can decide what time you have off and what time you don't?'

'That's not how big business is run,' he said, turning round to face her. 'If I'm not at the helm, the ship goes down.'

'Not for one day!'

They stared at each other, and she refused to lower her eyes first.

'Dammit,' he muttered finally, scowling at her, 'and what am I supposed to do with a five-year-old child for a day? Bake bread together? Play dolls?'

Katherine didn't say anything, but she realised that she must have looked aghast because he continued, with a certain amount of harsh defiance in his voice.

'I'm sure that entertaining children is easy for you, but I have no experience of doing that. And you don't have to give me that kind of look!' he suddenly roared, which made her jump.

'What kind of look?'

'The look that says that I'm a rotten father.' He strode across the kitchen and sat down at the table next to her. 'Claire has everything she wants or needs! More! She just has to say what she wants, and she gets it!'

'There's no need to justify yourself to me!' Katherine snapped. 'I was only making a suggestion.' She stared into the mesmerising sea-green eyes and had a sensation of drowning, which she hurriedly covered up by saying, 'I must be getting off now.' She stood up and wondered where she'd left her jacket. She didn't relish having to go through the bowels of the house looking.

'Sit down,' he commanded brusquely, and she hesitated, then sat down again.

This wasn't because she felt intimidated, she told herself, it was a matter of diplomacy. He was, after all, the fee-paying parent of one of her pupils, and for that reason she was obliged to listen to what he had to say. Telling herself that made her feel much better, and she looked at him with polite equanimity.

'Why the hell don't you just come right out with it? I can't stand these muted, accusing looks.'

'All right, then. Claire needs a father, not just someone who pays the bills and makes sure that her every wish is fulfilled, materially speaking. Children are very sensitive to things like that. A child who is showered with everything that money can buy but denied the one thing that it can't grows up into a very rebellious, very unfulfilled adult.'

'So now I'm potentially responsible for bringing a juvenile delinquent into the world, is that it?'

'Oh, forget it,' she sighed. 'There's no getting through to you, is there?'

'I haven't had a great deal of experience with Claire,' he admitted, with visible reluctance. He looked at her from under his thick, dark lashes. 'Her mother used her against me as revenge for the divorce. I was allowed to see her, but at times that suited her, and sometimes in situations that made it impossible for me to be relaxed with my daughter.'

'Why?' Katherine looked at him, astonished, and his lips twisted.

'Because that's the way of women, isn't it?'

'Not all women!' she protested.

'And you speak from the pinnacle of all that's good and saintly, do you?' There was sarcasm in his voice and she reddened.

'Don't drag me into your argument. If you want to send her off to the child-minder to get her out of your hair, then by all means go right ahead and do so.' She stood up and walked towards the sink with her cup. 'Now, if you don't mind, I really must get home.'

'Why? Is David waiting there for you?' He turned in his chair to look at her.

'No one is waiting there for me,' she answered coolly. 'But that doesn't mean that I plan on staying here and being insulted. Believe it or not, I would rather sit at home in my empty house and count cracks on the ceiling than do that.'

He got up and moved over to her swiftly, with feline grace.

'I'll just get my jacket,' she said warily.

'Oh, I'll get it for you.' He left the kitchen and returned a couple of minutes later with her jacket, which he held out for her. She would rather have shrugged it on herself, but she allowed him to help her with it, her body keenly aware of his.

He swivelled her round to face him and kept his hands on the collar of the jacket.

'Wouldn't you like to stay and have something to eat?' he asked, and she shook her head. That, she could have told him, without thinking too hard about it, was the last thing in the world she wanted. In fact, it probably ranked, alongside falling in a snake-pit, as one of the experiences she least needed in her life.

'Why not?' he asked, and there was a cruel smile on his mouth when he looked at her.

'I have food at home,' she said, a little unevenly.

'Sure that's the reason?'

'What other reason could there be?' There was sharp alarm in her voice, but she still did her best to keep her calm, to ignore the suffocating sensation that being so close to him evoked.

'Running scared, maybe?' He laughed. 'When you stormed round here to tell me how indifferent to me you were, I couldn't help thinking that it was a bit of an over-reaction.'

She should never have done that, she realised with a sinking feeling. She had forgotten how minutely sensitive Dominic Duvall was to the shades and nuances of people's behaviour.

'You flatter yourself,' she mumbled, and his hands moved from the collar of her jacket to the sides of her face, scorching through her skin, igniting a flame inside her which she knew would flicker out if only she could ignore it.

'Do I? Or maybe you are afraid that if you get too close to me, you might find your body doing things that your mind would much rather it didn't.'

'This is ludicrous. Please let me go.'

'Or else what?'

'Or else I shall kick you on the shin as hard as I can, and you'll be forced to stay at home then, with a heavily bandaged foot.'

'All that fire,' he murmured, 'underneath the prim clothes and the prim expression. Have you spent six years pouring water on it, hoping that it would go out?'

'I don't know what you're talking about, nor do I care.' Brave words, she thought. Shame that the incoherent confusion inside her gave the game away. At least to herself.

She cold feel herself trembling, a mixture of anger and terrible awareness of him, of that dark sexuality.

'You know,' he said.

'I'm a schoolteacher, Mr Duvall,' she began, and he laughed again, as though he found her protests very amusing indeed. 'I am not a fiery person!'

'Shall we put that to the test?' His mouth crushed hers, sending her head back, forcing her lips apart so that he could invade her with his tongue.

Katherine struggled against him and he kissed her harder, pinning her against the kitchen counter, devouring her.

She heard herself groan, a husky, shameful sound, and his hands left her face and sought the warmth of her body, pushing under her jumper, moving upwards until she felt them slide beneath the lacy cups of her bra, finding her breasts, releasing them from captivity.

They swelled into his hands, aching, throbbing, and he buried his mouth against her neck, so that her head fell back and her body arched in response to his searching fingers

She was barely thinking as he lifted her jumper, exposing her breasts, playing with them, then finally bending his head and flicking his tongue against the hard, raised nipples. Then he sucked harder, drawing first one nipple then the other into his mouth, while she lay back against the counter in an attitude of what was, even through her haze of blurred thinking, shocking abandon.

Her whole body hurt with the intensity of what was going through her, and she could feel the dampness between her legs, her wet arousal, with despair and mortification.

She pushed him away, but she was still shaking like a leaf as he drew back.

'No fire, Katherine?' he taunted, and she raised angry eyes to his.

'What satisfaction have you derived from this?' she asked.

'The satisfaction of knowing that I could take you if I wanted to. You walked away once, but now you could be my captive if I wanted. Don't you think that that's satisfaction enough?'

'I may be attracted to you still,' she whispered, horrified at that, 'but I could never be yours!'

'Never?' he smiled coolly. 'Be careful, little schoolteacher, you may find that the past has claws that could reach out and grab you, even now.'

CHAPTER SIX

THE Nativity play was going well. Rehearsals had been the usual joyous affair of dozens of young children engagingly trying their best to learn lines and remember words to songs.

With two weeks before the big day, and only three weeks to Christmas, the atmosphere was alight with excitement.

Normally, Katherine derived a great deal of pleasure from all this. She could remember as yesterday how lacking in sparkle Christmas had always been for her. She had always played her part in nativity plays as well, but her driving, childish desire to do it to perfection, so very well that perhaps this time her mother might unbend a little and cheer and smile from the audience, just like the other parents, had always made it a tense occasion for her. She would frown with concentration and try so hard that, in the end, the gay spontaneity would be lost and she would know, from her mother's expression, that she had failed yet again.

Now, as a teacher, she always found herself looking carefully at the faces, making sure that they were having fun, because having fun was what it was all about. It was rewarding, feeling their excitement, watching them in their red tights and amateurishly concocted elfin hats.

She looked around her now, but her thoughts were miles away.

Dominic Duvall had kissed her. That had been weeks

ago, but she couldn't seem to dislodge the episode from her mind. It hovered there, only a memory, but still as capable of damage as a high-explosive bomb.

Six years of rebuilding her life, and all for nothing. He had taken her in his arms and, even though the crushing force of his mouth had been lacking all tenderness or affection, it had been enough to send her hurtling back through time, back to when she had shed her inhibitions, back to when she had been a vulnerable, yearning pupil in his hands.

The rehearsal was coming to a close. A chaotic gathering of fifty or so pupils, ranging from under four to slightly over six, was lustily singing to the determined thumping of the music teacher on the piano.

The acoustics in the small hall were appalling. Even a choir of angels would find it hard going, and the unsynchronised children's voices were rendered completely tiny, but the teachers all clapped with great fervour afterwards, including Katherine, who had been so absorbed in her thoughts that she only surfaced when the crashing finale from the piano woke her up. Mrs Hale was a great believer in enthusiastic piano-playing. Her finales could have roused the dead.

Katherine spent the remainder of the day doing what she normally did, but without energy. Fortunately the children, without exception, failed to notice anything amiss. She wondered whether it was a great fallacy that young children were sensitive to atmosphere. Perhaps they really only tuned in to open displays of weeping and gnashing of teeth and wringing of hands.

She tried to imagine what it must be like to be absolutely carefree, and found that she couldn't. She couldn't even really imagine what it must be like to be marginally carefree. No problems except petty ones, like when to get the turkey, and whether Great-Aunt Dorothy's presence at the Christmas dinner was worth the glow of self-righteousness afterwards.

She herself viewed the swiftly approaching Christmas holidays with trepidation.

Usually she would make sure that she put up a tree, a real one, with all the trimmings, and she also made sure that she filled her time as much as she could with visiting friends.

But friends, at the moment, held no appeal, and she had no idea what she would do with herself on Christmas Day. Lunch with David and his mother, which had become something of a pleasant routine, looked doubtful.

He had told her, rather hesitantly and with some embarrassment, that he and Jack were trying to work out how they could spend the time together. He wanted her, he said, to meet his mother, but apparently that entailed staying in the area, and if they stayed in the area Dominic would expect her to join him. This appeared to be a consuming problem for him, far more consuming than all the work problems which had plagued his life in the past and about which he had told her in exhaustive detail. Now, whenever she spoke to him, which was infrequently, he brushed aside her questions about his job with the casual nonchalance of someone flapping away a fly.

Her mind changed gear, divided between the problem of Dominic and the problem of Christmas.

She was frowning as she left the school just after six-thirty, pulling her coat around her, head bent as she hurried towards her car.

The weather was, as usual, living down to most people's expectations, with bleak, leaden skies and freezing rain, and without even the erratic bursts of cold sunshine which only seemed to be glimpsed on Christmas cards.

She crashed into him so hard that she staggered back, with an automatic apology on her lips, before she looked up and saw who it was.

'Oh.' That was the only thing that she could find to say. In the wintry dark, Dominic was just a towering form, in his black overcoat, open at the front so that she could glimpse the dark suit underneath.

'I want to have a word with you,' he said, and she blinked.

'It's more orthodox to arrange a meeting at the school,' Katherine said, shifting her eyes to the less disturbing vista of her car, one of the last in the car park.

'This isn't about Claire.'

'I see.' She cleared her throat and looked longingly at the car.

'Perhaps we could have a meal somewhere.'

'A meal?' She hoped that the inky blackness was hiding the look of horror on her face.

She had had weeks to put things in perspective, weeks to realise that she was still as attracted to him as she had ever been, weeks to come to terms with the fact that her attraction was forbidden, a dangerous seed which could not be allowed to grow because it would take over her life like ivy climbing up a wall.

'Where can we go to eat around here?' he asked impatiently. 'Where's your car?'

'Over there.' She pointed vaguely at the car park and side-stepped him. Her black patent shoes, with their sensible heels, clicked on the path. He walked beside her, softly, like a shadow.

'I'm afraid—' she began, slipping the key into the lock and not looking at him.

'I'll follow you back to your house and wait for you there.'

'My house?'

'No need to panic,' he said with the same impatient drawl, 'you'll be quite safe. I won't jump on you from behind the curtains.'

'Very funny,' Katherine muttered tightly.

'Let's get moving.'

'I'm busy tonight,' she said rudely.

'Not now, you're not. I'll be behind you.'

He walked off to his car, started the engine and waited while she clambered into hers and drove out of the car park with her mind in utter disarray.

What did he want to talk about? If not his daughter, then what? Surely not about them. That subject had now been resoundingly closed.

She glanced in the mirror and saw his car, long and powerful, silently following, and tried to stanch the sudden dreadful anticipation gnawing away at her.

She didn't want him in her house, she didn't want to have a meal with him, she didn't want even to look at him. He had been right. She was absolutely terrified at what she felt whenever he was around. She was terrified at the way she lost her grip on reality; she was terrified that he would see her vulnerability.

But she couldn't stop him, short of losing him down one of the dimly lit side-streets, and, anyway, he knew where she lived.

So she made her way miserably back to her house, stuck a composed expression on her face as she got out of her car and then, once they were inside, she said, slipping off her coat, 'There's no need to take me out for a meal. You can say whatever you want to say right here. I can make us some coffee.'

'A meal would be so much more civilised, though, wouldn't it? Why don't you go and change?'

He had stuck his hands in the pockets of his coat and was looking at her politely.

'All right,' she said with reluctance, and vanished into her bedroom, making sure to lock the door behind her, but very quietly. She wasn't going to invite any more insulting, humorous asides at her expense.

She had a shower, changed into a neat navy blue suit, which, like everything else in her wardrobe, could comfortably fit into the category of self-effacing and went back into the lounge, where he had directed his attention to her books, an inordinate number of them, which were squeezed into several shelves in one of the alcoves by the fireplace.

'I'm ready,' she said briskly, and he turned to look at her.

'Haven't you got anything less formal?' he asked, and she could tell from his tone of voice that he was distinctly unimpressed with her choice.

'There's nothing wrong with this suit,' Katherine said defensively.

'No.' He shrugged and walked towards the door. 'What happened,' he asked, turning round to her with his hand on the door-knob, 'to all those clothes you wore in London?'

Borrowed plumage, she could have told him. Instead she said shortly, 'I burnt them.'

'You burnt them?'

'Metaphorically speaking.'

'Why? Were you so bitter at your boyfriend's rejection?'

'Something like that,' she answered, and he turned away, opening the door and walking towards his car.

She slipped into the passenger seat and obligingly discussed restaurants, but her knowledge of them was limited to the cheaper variety and, as she expected, he ignored them all and drove to an expensive Italian restaurant which she had heard of but had never visited. On a teacher's salary, luxurious dining out was not a matter of course. On her birthdays David had always taken her out, but to local bistros, where the music tended to be over loud and the food cheap and cheerful.

'I'm not dressed for a place like this,' she said to Dominic, as they waited to be seated.

'You shouldn't have burnt your clothes,' he told her shortly. 'Metaphorically speaking, of course. I never knew a woman who voluntarily got rid of designer clothes so that she could run out and buy a wardrobe full of suits.'

'Not among the women you know, at any rate,' Katherine muttered under her breath.

The restaurant was small, intimate, with candles and flowers on the tables, and waiters who appeared to have taken degrees in subservience.

They were ushered like royalty to a table in the corner of the room, half hidden by an exotic-looking plant, and as soon as they had sat down, she said, 'Now, what was it that you wanted to discuss?'

'What happened to your friend in London?' Dominic asked, ordering drinks for both of them and, to her surprise, remembering precisely what she had liked—white wine with soda water.

'I still keep in touch with her,' Katherine said, shrugging and playing with the stem of her wine-glass.

Not quite a complete lie. They did still keep in touch, but only via the occasional letter and Christmas cards. Twice, Emma had come to visit, but country life bored her and she had spent the entire time trying to rouse Katherine's interest in returning to the much more exciting playground of London.

'Well, it's heartening to know that she didn't go the way of the clothes,' Dominic murmured, and she looked at him warily from under her lashes.

'I don't suppose you came here to discuss me.' Back to the brisk tone of voice. It was the one she felt most in control with.

'Why do you suppose that?'

The waiter handed them their menus, great, ornate things, which looked as though they should have far more important contents than descriptions of food.

'Because I am a very boring subject.' She was busy scanning the menu and didn't realise that he hadn't answered until she looked up at him and found that he was staring at her.

'What makes you say that?'

'Does it matter?' she asked, a little taken aback. 'I think I'll have the sole.'

'Was that the reason your boyfriend gave you when he walked out on you?'

'I don't want to discuss all that. It's in the past.'

'Exactly,' he said smoothly, coolly, 'so why should it bother you if we discuss it or not? Why do you think that you're boring? You had a great deal more self-confidence when I knew you. You didn't continually act as though you were running away from something.'

'Everyone's running away from something,' she muttered ambiguously, and when he raised his eyebrows she continued irritably, 'You don't give up do you? All right, I'm not boring, I'm vastly exciting, with my wardrobe of suits and my early nights and my sensible job!' She knew that she sounded bitter and she hated the way he had managed to draw this heated response out of her when she had spent thirty-five minutes in the car rehearsing her composure.

'Well, well, well.' He sat back and looked at her with such undiluted concentration that she began to feel jumpy and defensive and hot under the collar.

'I know what you're thinking.' She gave him a chance to jump in here and conduct a little psychoanalysis on her, but he remained silent, which propelled her into more murky waters. 'I'm really quite a self-confident person.'

'You must be,' he agreed, 'to hold down a job like the one you do. Children soon see through someone who's not at ease with them.'

Katherine laughed, an open, honest sound. 'I'm not entirely sure about that. At the age of four and five, they're far more concerned with what's happening around them than they are with the mental state of their teacher. They're also terribly trusting. The urge to take advantage of people's weaknesses comes later, I think.'

'Is Claire finding it hard going?' he asked, looking at her intently.

That was something she had forgotten over the years, the way he could give his undivided attention to whatever was being said to him.

'She did to start with, I think,' Katherine said, pausing while their food was elaborately laid in front of them, then continuing between mouthfuls of sole and vegetables. 'She speaks English very fluently, but her mind just didn't work fast enough sometimes to catch on to what the other children were saying. Now, she's marvellous. Not boisterous, but then, I don't think that she'll ever be, do you?'

'No,' Dominic said thoughtfully. 'She's always been quite an introverted child.'

'Yes. I know. I can sympathise.' She stood back and looked at what she had just said, and then murmured, unwillingly drawn into confiding, 'I was quite the same. My father left home when I was very young, and my mother...' She paused. She never spoke about her mother to anyone. She had internalised all the problems she had endured and had always made the best of them. It was only in later years that she had been able to realise how much things had affected her.

'Your mother…?' There was interest there, but not pressing, and she plunged on.

'My mother resented my father's leaving. She always maintained that he had abandoned us, which of course he had, but…'

'She blamed you?'

'No.'

'She made you pay for his desertion?'

'Something like that.' Katherine laughed nervously. 'I told you I was a terribly boring person.'

'You never really discussed your past with me all those years ago,' he murmured, 'did you?'

Katherine met his eyes steadily and said with utter truthfulness, 'When I met you, I had no past and no future.'

'Tell me,' Dominic said, and there was a latent urgency in his voice that unsettled her.

'Tell you what?'

'Tell me what you're hiding.'

She lowered her eyes. She could feel the fine prickle of perspiration. Tell him? she thought. The truth? The long, involved truth that had cost her so dear? He had said that the past no longer mattered because what they had had was finished, that two strangers who had briefly crossed paths no longer needed secrets, but she felt otherwise. He might have eliminated her from his life, but she was honest enough to realise that she had never managed to do the same to him. It was pointless trying to analyse what, precisely, she did feel for him, but she knew that it certainly wasn't the indifference which she would have needed if she were to suddenly plunge into a polite, amusing confession of things that had happened six years ago.

'I'm not hiding anything,' she said, keeping her eyes lowered.

'Were you involved with the two of us at the same time?' he asked, with a sharp narrowing of his eyes which belied the mild curiosity in his voice. 'Did you get pregnant by him?'

Katherine looked at him, startled, then she laughed, throwing her head back, leaning back into the chair.

'Do share the joke,' Dominic said coldly, and her laughter subsided into bursts of giggles.

'I have never been pregnant in my life,' she said, thinking that pregnancy by a fictitious lover would certainly have guaranteed her a place in the *Guinness Book of Records*. 'That is the most absurd suggestion I have ever heard in my entire life.' Which made him frown even more. 'Have you ever thought of going into writing fiction?'

'Very droll, Katherine,' he muttered, unamused, judging from the look on his face.

'I don't know why you feel the need to get to the bottom of all this,' she said seriously. 'I suppose it has something to do with male pride, but I have no intention of satisfying your urge to fit the pieces of the puzzle together. I mean, would you ever have wondered at all if chance hadn't made us meet once again?'

'Unfinished business never goes away,' he said, signalling to the waiter for the coffee. He leaned towards her. 'And the fact is that we have met once again, and I won't give up until I've worked out what motivated you then and what motivates you now.'

She looked at him with alarm.

'Why? What would you gain from that?'

'Satisfaction, Katherine.' He sat back, and when he smiled there was the promise lurking there that he meant every word he had said.

That frightened her even more than if he had admitted that he needed to find out what had gone wrong so suddenly six years ago because of sheer, naked curiosity, because the way he said it spoke of something very impersonal, very cold. A detached desire to work it all out in the same way that he might feel the desire to solve a complicated intellectual enigma.

He had ceased being interested in her a long time ago, and certainly the woman sitting here now in front of him meant nothing at all to him, but there was a ruthless logic about him that would not permit this enigma to pass by unravelled.

The waiter approached and asked the usual questions about whether they had enjoyed the meal or not. Katherine wondered what he would do if she stood up and said that she hadn't. Would it ruffle that efficient, mask-like courteousness? Would he throw his hands up in horror? Would he drag the chef out and demand a full explanation of what had gone wrong?

It was all a technicality, anyway, because the food had been very good, and even if it had been totally inedible she would have bitten back the criticism. She had had too many years of self-effacement ever to indulge voluntarily in histrionics.

'Why do you think Claire is so introverted, as you put it?' she asked him suddenly, and he answered immediately, as though the abrupt shift in their conversation was not at all disconcerting.

'A reaction to her mother's personality, I should think,' he said smoothly. 'Françise was a very flamboyant woman. She tended to overshadow most people, and that included her daughter.'

'Is that why you married her?' Katherine asked carefully. 'Because she was flamboyant?'

'I married her because she was pregnant.'

He sipped some of his coffee and stared at her over the cup, as though awaiting her next question with some amusement. She knew that he would answer her only if he wanted to, and if she overstepped the mark he would simply, coolly and very abruptly, stop.

She realised with a jolt that if he hadn't known her, then she had not really known him either. For six months they had existed on a sort of surreal plane of pleasure. It seemed unreal that something so short could have been so powerful and could have had such far-reaching consequences.

'Poor Claire,' she said with sympathy. It was all she could find to say. She might have wanted to ask him more, ask him about himself, but that game of courtship was not one in which she was free to indulge. Teachers could ask so much and no more, and personal questions were forbidden by some general, unspoken code of ethics.

'We've finished eating,' she said instead, 'and you still haven't told me why you asked me here in the first place.'

'So I haven't.' He sat back, folded his arms and said silkily, 'I want to know what's going on with my sister.'

'Your sister?' Katherine looked at him with surprise. 'Why on earth should I know what's going on with your sister?'

'Because she seems to like you. If she had needed to confide in someone, you probably would have fitted the bill.'

What a staggering compliment, Katherine thought acidly. Dull enough to fit the bill as eternal confidante to the masses. Opiate of other people's emotional headaches, the human equivalent of an aspirin.

'If your sister had confided in me, then I'd hardly be likely to tell all to you, would I?' she retorted.

'Has she told you what the hell is going on?' he asked,

as though she hadn't spoken. She developed a taste for going out at night, which isn't unusual for my sister, but it's quite unusual in that I don't see any of these so-called friends she's going out with.'

'Why should it worry you if she goes out, for heaven's sake?' Katherine asked, perplexed. 'She's not a child.'

'From what I can see, she's hardly an adult either.'

'Maybe you should look a bit harder.'

The waiter glided over with the bill, and while Dominic paid she tried to fathom out where his suspicions were leading, because they were leading somewhere.

'Jack,' he said, resuming their conversation in the car as though there had been no lapse in between, 'is high-spirited. Too high-spirited for her own good.'

'That's no bad thing,' Katherine murmured, thinking back to her own youth. Maybe if she had been high-spirited then, she would not have felt that desperate urge to throw everything to the winds when events began snowballing.

'She's also extremely gullible,' Dominic said from next to her.

'And so you see it as your duty to steer her away from temptation.'

'I see it as my duty to make sure that she doesn't land herself in a situation from which she might find it impossible to extricate herself.' His voice was hard.

They had reached her house, and she opened her door and said, in a winding-up sort of voice, 'Well, I'm sure that she can take very good care of herself.' She headed up the path to her front door, and with a sinking heart heard his door slam behind him.

'I want to know if she has told you anything,' he said, following her into the house and proceeding to settle himself on the sofa in the sitting-room as though he had every right in the world to be there.

'Not a thing,' Katherine informed him truthfully. 'Not one single thing. And I can't imagine what good it is going to do if you now decide to put the bloodhounds on her trail. She has to be allowed to live her own life.'

'Is that what they teach you in your teacher training courses?' he asked with a hint of derision.

'No, I think it's called common sense. Over-protect someone and sooner or later they're going to rebel against it, whereas if you just let them live their own lives, they'll learn from their mistakes and arrive at the right conclusions in the end.'

'What a trusting philosophy of life,' he said curtly, which made her hackles rise.

'She won't appreciate it if you decide to start quizzing her on her every movement. Can't you see that? There are some things in life that you can't control.'

'I will not allow her to do anything foolish,' he said with utter calm.

'I'm sure she won't,' Katherine murmured, refusing to be needled into an argument. 'And even if she does, does it matter? It's inevitable, isn't it?'

'You don't seem to understand,' he said coldly. 'Any mistake that Jack makes could turn out to be a very costly one indeed.'

'So it all comes down to money, does it?' she asked. 'You're not all that bothered by your sister's emotional welfare. What really bothers you is that she could end up costing you money.'

He threw her a glance of brooding impatience. 'Stop being deliberately naïve. It's obvious that my sister is involved with a man, and it's equally obvious that he's undesirable, because she hasn't seen fit to bring him home.'

'For you to inspect,' she murmured. 'Frankly, I can understand why.'

He looked at her savagely, then stood up and began pacing the room.

'Is she going out with that David fellow?' he asked eventually, and she drew her breath in.

'What on earth makes you think that she is?'

'Who else? She used to mention him, now she doesn't. Are you seeing him?'

'Of course I am,' she said uncomfortably. 'Anyway, why would David be a threat to her? Or, for that matter, any upright, dependable type like him?'

'No one's dependable when it comes to money,' he answered scathingly. 'I want to know whether he's seeing my sister.'

'Ask him,' she replied, which made his face darken with fury.

'I'm asking you!'

'And I am not a child to be bullied!' she replied in a high, angry voice. 'David and I are still very close.' Oh, God, why have I been dragged into this? 'And he's not the sort to play the field with more than one woman at a time.' That, as it went, and taken out of context, was the truth. Technically, she said to herself, I'm not lying.

'Since when?'

'I'm not about to argue with you.' She jumped up from where she was sitting and walked towards the front door. 'Thank you for a very nice meal. Now, if you don't mind, I'd be grateful if you leave.'

She positioned herself by the front door and he sauntered up to her and lounged against the wall, staring down at her.

'Are you so sure that you know this David chap of yours?' he asked silkily. 'The last time I laid eyes on him he was vanishing with my sister and assuring everyone within hearing distance that the two of you were only good friends.'

'That's an exaggeration,' Katherine replied uneasily.

'Or maybe you prefer to pretend to yourself that it is? Maybe you just don't want to face the unpalatable truth that your success with the opposite sex leaves something to be desired. Six months of game-playing with me years ago, only to discover that it was all in vain and the response you wanted from your lover never materialised. He vanished, and now David. It must be frustrating for you.'

'David hasn't vanished,' she snapped, knowing that angry, embarrassed colour had flooded into her face.

'So you're still seeing each other, are you? He has nothing to do with my sister?'

'Stop trying to squeeze answers out of me.'

'Face facts. He's not interested in you, Katherine. He's probably cavorting who knows where even as was speak with Jack.'

His voice was cold and merciless and she could feel herself drowning in the depths of his eyes, floundering about like a fish out of water.

'What do you want me to say?' she asked shakily. 'That everything you say is true? That I'm a desperate woman who will do anything to believe that the man she loves isn't seeing someone else?'

'You love him, do you?'

'Of course I love him.' But not in the way you think. I love him the way I would love a brother, the brother I never had. I love him the way I would love a friend, someone who has been around for years and has taken the trouble to listen when I had something to say. Yes, that's how I love him. But I don't love him as a man. I don't love him with the burning, painful, driving passion that makes sense of everything and yet still manages to turn everything upside-down. No, that love isn't for David. That love is all for you.

The recognition didn't surprise her. It wasn't something that had crept up on her slowly until she was forced to acknowledge it. No, she had loved him then, and she had never stopped, and deep down she had known that.

From the minute he had walked into that schoolroom, and she had looked up to see the face that had haunted her dreams for six years, she had known.

She looked away with deep misery and he caught her face between his hands. There was a blazing anger in his eyes.

'Stop lying to yourself, Katherine,' he said sharply. 'You don't love him any more than he loves you.'

'And you're suddenly a mind-reader, are you?'

'You forget that I know you.'

'You only think you do.' She drew a deep breath and tried not to let her face reflect her thoughts. Everything was so muddled, so horribly confused. The only clear, unalterable fact shining through was that her love for Dominic Duvall was not part of any equation. 'What would you do, anyway? If David was seeing your sister?'

'It would depend on how serious it was.'

He was still staring at her, thinking thoughts she could not begin to guess at. There was something savage and intense in his eyes, an angry stillness in his body that alarmed and excited her. She looked down, shaking.

'And if it was very serious?'

'Are you trying to tell me something?'

'I am only speaking hypothetically.'

'Then,' he said, without a shade of uncertainty, 'hypothetically speaking, I would be obliged to do everything in my power to end it. I intend to protect my sister from fortune-hunters, and an impoverished schoolteacher, unhappy in his job, would fit that description with no trouble at all.' He straightened up, and when he looked at her his face was dark with menace. 'So, if you're protecting him for some reason, then you're a fool. And if you're not, if you actually believe that the two of you have any sort of future together, then you, my dear Katherine, are an even bigger fool.'

CHAPTER SEVEN

OF COURSE, and with an ever-increasing feeling of sinking into a quagmire, Katherine told David about Dominic's visit and, with untypical jauntiness, he dismissed everything she said with a flourish.

In fact, and she thought about this later, there was a worrying excitement about him. If she hadn't known better, she would have thought that he was coming down with something. Flu, perhaps, or maybe a bout of temporary insanity, if temporary insanity manifested itself in a disturbing, feverish brightness.

When she told him that perhaps he should be sensible, try and make sure that Jack was more at home with Dominic, he laughed. When she told him that Dominic could be a formidable opponent, he laughed even harder and told her to stop worrying, to stop acting like an old woman, which hurt her more than she let him see.

Well, she silently informed the exercise book, staring at her with its gay drawing of a lop-sided Christmas tree and a Santa Claus who defied the rules of gravity and appeared to be suspended somewhere in mid-air, don't say that I didn't try. I hereby wash my hands of the whole sorry matter.

Except that she had an uneasy feeling that the whole sorry matter hadn't washed its hands of her. Not yet. And she was right, because two days later, not fifteen minutes after she had arrived back, and just as she was thinking about fixing herself something to eat, the doorbell went, and she knew, with a feeling of resignation, that the sorry matter was about to appear on her doorstep.

She knew that it would be David even before she opened the door. Or maybe Jack. Or more likely both of them, with more plans to ensconce her in their convoluted love-affair.

She would refuse, she decided. She would put her foot down, and to hell with it if they thought that she was a fuddy-duddy.

She yanked open the door and froze when she saw Dominic standing outside, dressed in a dinner jacket, complete with a bow tie.

'Stop looking as though I'm from another planet,' he said, with his usual endearing lack of preliminaries, 'and let me in.'

'You've come to the wrong house,' Katherine told him, not budging. 'There's no party here.'

'I have no time for amusing games,' he said, brushing past her and then shutting the door before she could say anything. 'I need a favour from you. And don't,' he added, 'even think about listing excuses.'

'What favour?' She was trying hard not to stare, but she couldn't seem to help herself. Dressed like that, his sexuality was overpowering. She couldn't remember a time when she had ever seen a man look quite so devastatingly handsome.

'I have a client do tonight and Jack has let me down.' His voice was flat and grim. 'When I get my hands on her, I am personally going to wring her neck.'

'You want me to go in her place?' Was that her voice? It sounded more like a squeak.

'Right the first time.'

'But why me?' she asked, staring at him with horror.

'Haven't you got anyone else you could ask? Anyone suitable?'

'You are eminently suitable. Now, I know that this is an invasion of your privacy, and for that I apologise, but Jack's sudden disappearance has left me no choice.' He didn't sound in the slightest apologetic, and she felt the sharp tang of tears well up. Why was it that everyone took her for granted? Now even he was assuming that she would have no hesitation in helping him out of a difficult situation.

'I'm afraid I have nothing to wear,' she said, not even bothering with the charade of pretending that she had other things on her agenda. 'I really haven't, Dominic.'

He looked at her for a while, a long look that made her want to die of embarrassment.

What was he seeing? she wondered. A woman, not so young any more, living a life so devoid of high excitement that there was nothing in her wardrobe that could take her anywhere really dressy. He was probably measuring her up against the woman he had known, in her borrowed plumage, who had danced till dawn and laughed until her eyes watered.

'Let me have a look,' he said abruptly.

'I'm not lying to you.'

'Where is your bedroom?'

She glanced up the stairs and hesitated, and in that fleeting second of hesitation he started up, with her following behind and feeling thoroughly sorry for herself.

He pulled open the doors of the wardrobe while she hovered miserably in the background, feeling ashamed rather than enraged.

It was funny, she knew, but when she had spent those six months in London, she had dressed in clothes she would never have dreamt of buying for herself, and she hadn't felt at all uncomfortable because it had all been like an extended version of play-acting. And, in an odd way, the clothes had dictated her personality to some extent. They had made her look vivacious and self-confident, and she had behaved accordingly.

But the minute she had left that all behind it had been as though she had returned to being Cinderella without her finery. She had invested in plain, unexciting clothes. She had, she realised, resumed the character which had been moulded by her mother, who had only ever bought her plain, unexciting clothes.

Dominic flicked through the wardrobe, pulled out a black skirt and jacket and then turned to her and asked if she had any lacy black camisoles.

'Well, yes,' Katherine stammered, red-faced.

'Wear one.'

'With what over it?'

'Nothing. Just your jacket.' He smiled a smile of utter charm, and when she emerged half an hour later she had to admit that she felt very different from what she had imagined. She had also left her hair loose, and it hung down her back in a straight, glossy sheet. She had looked in the mirror in her bedroom and had found it difficult to believe that this was really her.

'That's better.' He nodded appreciatively. 'Now, if you could just look a little more relaxed, then we might be getting somewhere.'

'I don't normally dress like this,' she told him in the car, which was chauffeur-driven so that he could drink without having to think about driving back.

'I won't bother to remind you that you did. Once.' She knew that he was looking at her averted face. 'For some reason you believe that that was not really you, that you are a thoroughly unadventurous woman.'

'I *am*,' she said stubbornly. Her hands were balled into

clenched fists and she could feel her naked breasts pushing against the lacy material.

'And I take it that this all harks back to the mother who made you feel responsible for her own failure to make her marriage work?'

Katherine shot him an astonished, nervous glance out of the corner of her eye.

'I was a mousy child,' she whispered, thinking that this was hardly a conversation they should be having, least of all in a car.

He wasn't interested in her, she knew that, and she wished that he wouldn't ask her questions.

'Is that what your mother said?'

'In combination with the bedroom mirror,' Katherine said with a laugh, but he didn't laugh back. The angular lines of his face were hard.

'And what did it feel like when you finally did let your hair down in London?'

It was the first time he had mentioned their time together without that angry edge of bitterness, or else cold indifference, and she said thoughtfully, looking at him, 'Wonderful.' She could remember the recklessness that had taken her over the minute she had made her decision. All her fear and bewilderment and rage had left, and she had thrown herself into that life with a demonic, driving intensity which she had never felt before.

'It was liberating,' she continued, watching him but not really seeing him because she was too wrapped up in seeing back into herself. 'It was as though someone had waved a magic wand and released me from a cage. Well, no, that sounds as though I had been desperately unhappy before, but I hadn't.' She gave a self-conscious laugh under her breath. 'It was as though a door had been opened.'

'I rest my case,' Dominic said brusquely, and she looked at him, puzzled.

'What case?'

'Figure it out for yourself.' The car was pulling up outside a hotel, and Katherine felt a fluttering of nerves. She sneaked a quick look at Dominic, who was leaning forward to say something to the chauffeur, and who looked as though any nerves he might ever have possessed had long since solidified into steel.

This whole situation, she thought, was peculiar. What was she doing, going along with Dominic Duvall to an expensive hotel in the centre of Birmingham to entertain clients? She was neither his employee nor his mistress. Come to think of it, she was hard-pressed to describe precisely what she was.

A last resort, she told herself. Which was fine for him, but not for her, because whereas he had nothing to lose in casually turning up on her doorstep and asking her a favour, she had a great deal to lose.

He ushered her into the hotel, his hand lightly resting under her elbow, and she soon realised that the nerve-racking party she had expected was in fact only a group of six—three high-powered businessmen and their wives.

The businessmen, financiers of the highest order, were impeccably well-bred and looked slightly tired, as though being at the top of the pecking order was a wearying business indeed. Their wives, attired in very expensive clothes, with very expensive jewellery, instinctively broke away from their husbands, who discussed business over their pre-dinner drinks. They smiled a lot at Katherine, and asked her questions about herself, and wondered, she knew, what her relationship with Dominic Duvall was, although they were all too polite to ask outright.

It was, as it happened, a very pleasant evening. Her

nerves fizzled out before they even sat down at the table, and she found herself talking about her job honestly and engagingly. They all seemed to think that she was doing something really rather useful with her life, which made her laugh, but not without some pleasure.

The three other women there didn't have jobs. They appeared to spend their time doing various charitable deeds, decorating their houses, bringing up children and spending their husbands' hard-earned money.

'It wouldn't suit me at all,' Katherine murmured later, drowsily, when they were driving back in the car. She hadn't drunk a great deal, but she felt quite light-headed nevertheless, pleasantly light-headed. She had expected to spend the evening fraught with nerves but, although she was constantly aware of Dominic's presence at the table across from her, she had been too busy talking to let that worry away at her. It was so easy to let herself slip back into this love, she thought, and it would be all too dangerously easy to let him sense that.

She closed her eyes with a little sigh.

'Why not?' he asked curiously.

'I suppose I've become used to being a work-horse,' she said, laughing. 'Being at the beck and call of demanding children. I've become addicted to the exhaustion that comes with it.'

'You must have time off,' Dominic said with a trace of astonishment. 'What do you do during the school holidays? Do you go abroad?'

That made her laugh again. 'I went to Italy a couple of years ago. David and I stayed with a friend of a friend of a friend.' She smiled at the memory. It had been a good holiday, her first since she had walked out on Dominic, and although David had tried to persuade her to sleep with him she had been adamant, and he had obligingly conceded.

In retrospect, she could see now that his acquiescence had had more to do with a basic lack of attraction than with a polite respect for her refusals. They had always enjoyed the good friendship of two basically compatible, basically lonely people, who had interests in common.

'Oh, yes, David.' There was thick disapproval in his voice and she wondered whether she should try and elaborate on David's good points, because really, sooner or later, if he and Jack continued their romance, Dominic would have no choice but to accept him.

'Apart from Italy,' she said, deciding to change the subject, 'I haven't been on holiday anywhere. I don't get paid the earth,' she continued without rancour, 'and there always seems to be something more worth while to spend my money on rather than a two-week vacation.' Her eyes were closed but she knew that he was staring at her.

'And you don't crave the attraction of foreign shores?' he drawled.

'Not crave, no.' She looked out of the window and saw that it was beginning to snow, light feathery flakes that fell like powder from the sky. Maybe it would be a white Christmas. 'I'd like to see places, of course I would—who wouldn't? But I can't see the point in craving for what I can't have.' In the darkness of the car she smiled an ironic little smile and wished that her heart could take that piece of sensible advice and apply it to the man sitting alongside her. 'Besides—' she slanted her eyes across to him '—I grew up without holidays abroad. There was never the money to spare, and even if there was, Mother would probably have seen that as a waste.'

'What an austere view of life.'

'That's easy for you to say,' Katherine told him sharply. 'You've always had wealth to cushion you.'

'Was there ever a man, Katherine?' he asked softly, his

voice cool and only mildly curious. 'Or did you walk out because you felt inadequate?'

She felt her heart speed up, the way it always did whenever the past was mentioned.

'I never felt inadequate,' she answered truthfully. Many things, she thought, but not inadequate. Ashamed, deceitful, despairing, but never inadequate.

'And what are you going to do for the Christmas holidays?' he asked politely. She looked at him staring out of the window, his jaw clenched. It was as though the past stood savagely between them, raising its grinning head whenever they spent too long interacting like civilised adults. She wished that she could stretch out her hand and tell him everything, unburden herself of her secret, have him accept the reasons why she had done what she did, go back in time and make everything all right. She shook herself free of that wild daydream.

'I have no idea,' she said lightly.

'What do you usually do?'

'Spend it with David and his mother. She does a wonderful Christmas lunch.' She tried to make her voice happy and carefree.

'And why not this year?'

'Oh, I shall probably do the same,' she said vaguely. 'Cooking a turkey for one isn't such a good idea, is it? It would take me weeks to eat the leftovers!' There was an uneasy tension in the air. 'Claire told me that you've got a wonderful Christmas tree, which she decorated all by herself. She's very proud. Have you bought her presents yet?' If she could keep the conversation on a light basis, she thought, they might yet end the evening on a reasonably calm note, and by keeping it light she meant avoiding all mention of David and all mention of any relationship they had had in the past.

'I sent my secretary out to get them yesterday,' he told her, 'and before I get a lecture on lack of parental participation, I was merely following what Claire wrote out on her list.'

'I wasn't about to give you a lecture!' Katherine said, stung, because it reminded her too clearly of what David had said about her being an old woman. Was she really like that? 'What did she ask for?'

'An A4 list of toys, basically,' Dominic said, his dark face breaking into an amused smile. 'Television advertising has an awful lot to answer for.'

'And peer pressure,' Katherine said, relaxing.

'At that age?' he asked with a laugh.

'You'd be surprised.'

The car was drawing up the little lane to her cottage and she thought, for once, how dark and uninviting it looked. She wondered with a pang what it would be like to spend the rest of her life coming back to a house where there was no shared warmth and laughter, and she immediately told herself not to be foolish, that she was very lucky compared with a great many people who didn't have what she had.

Your greatest sorrow, a little voice said, is that you *know* what you could have had, isn't it? You had your glimpse of what it could have been like, but you were powerless to accept it.

'It was a lovely evening,' she said, gathering up her little bag and turning to him in the car. 'I hope you have a wonderful Christmas with Claire. She's just at that special age, when it's all so magical.'

The car stopped and she turned away.

'I'll see you inside,' Dominic said, opening his door and slipping out and, much as she would have liked to tell him that she was quite capable of seeing herself inside, she kept silent and shrugged.

The place was in complete darkness. She should have left a light on; it was what she usually did if she went out at night, but she must have forgotten. It had all been so sudden and nerve-racking.

She would have missed it, she realised later, if Dominic hadn't turned and switched on the main light in the hall. Normally Katherine turned on the little lamp on the table just by the door, where the telephone was. It gave off a much gentler glow.

With the bright hall light on, though, she couldn't miss the little white envelope lying just on the doormat. In fact, she almost stepped on it.

'Love-letter, perhaps?' Dominic's deep voice said from behind her.

'Circular, more likely,' Katherine replied, moving away and slitting open the envelope. There was no writing on the outside and she had no idea who it could be from, apart from an advertising company telling her about some new wondrous product or other, just the thing for Christmas, or else a charity asking for a donation of some sort or another.

It was from neither. Her eyes scanned the few lines, re-read them more carefully, then she looked up at Dominic with a shocked expression on her face.

'What is it?' His voice was like a whip and he moved across to her and grasped both her arms. 'What's the matter?'

'Read it,' she said in a low, shaky voice and he took the note from her and turned away.

It felt as though she stood there, in the cold hall, for hours, looking at that averted back, fearing the reaction to come, but it could have only been a few seconds, then Dominic was staring at her, his green eyes blazingly angry.

'The bastard,' he said, with a control in his voice which

was far more frightening than if he had exploded in rage and started throwing things about.

'Dominic,' she said hesitantly, 'please…' She took a step towards him, and his hand snapped around her wrist.

'You are coming with me,' he said grimly. 'I will not allow this!'

Oh, David, she thought with a wave of anger, how *could* you?

Dominic was pulling her back towards the door, taking the key from her, locking the house behind him, and she allowed herself to be led to the car, her mind a mass of whirling thoughts that bumped into each other, then whirled away again before sense could be made.

She should have foreseen something like this, she thought with confused worry. When she had last spoken to David, there had been something odd about his behaviour, something reckless, and, thinking back, she could see that it was the recklessness of a deed anticipated.

She glanced up into the rear-view mirror and the chauffeur's eyes quickly moved back to the road. What must he be thinking? she wondered. Me, white and shaken, and Dominic, barely containing a rage so powerful that it was frightening. She didn't dare look at him but she could feel the threat exuding from his body as though it was tangible.

They didn't say a word for the whole drive to his house.

What on earth could have possessed David, she thought, sensible, easygoing David, to do something as dramatic as this? Running off with Jack so that they could get married.

She recalled the note.

You weren't in, and I wanted you to know that Jack and I have decided to get married. We're sneaking off like thieves in the night because she's so damned afraid that her brother will do everything in his power to stop us if we make this all public. Should I be sorry? I don't feel sorry. I feel as though I'm in the clouds! Can you imagine what old Peck at the school will say? I will be in touch, of course, my dear Katherine!

Stunned, she thought. I feel utterly stunned. She controlled the desire to giggle hysterically.

'Come on,' said Dominic tightly, as soon as they had reached his house.

Once they were inside, the baby-sitter was dispatched with such speed that she looked quite bewildered, then he turned to her and said briefly, 'I'm going to have a whisky. Do you want one?'

Katherine shook her head and followed him into the kitchen, where, propped up against one of the counters, was a white envelope remarkably similar to the one that had been awaiting her on the doormat. Dominic ripped it open, read the contents and threw it into the bin.

'What does she say?' Katherine asked, not really seeing how she could avoid the question.

'"Darling brother,"—' his lips twisted crookedly as he quoted this '—"running away at my great age! Isn't it exciting? I shall be a married woman when next we meet and I hope that you'll have calmed down in the meanwhile. See you soon!" Dammit! Exciting! Running away on a little adventure and feeling as though she's a heroine in a children's book! Now can you see what I mean when I say that she's totally irresponsible?'

She watched in silence as he drank the contents of the glass in one gulp, then she followed him into the sitting-room, wishing desperately that she wasn't caught up in the middle of this drama, wishing that David had not run off and unwittingly left her embroiled in this mess.

'Now,' he said, standing by the Victorian fireplace and

looking at her, 'you know him—where do you think they've gone? Back to his place? Where does he live?'

'If they've made up their minds,' Katherine said carefully, 'then I don't think that it's a good idea for you to race around behind them so that you can try and stop it.'

It wasn't what he wanted to hear. His face was thunderous and she had to steel herself not to cringe back. This wasn't her fault, she told herself, and she wasn't going to act as though she had anything to hide or be ashamed of.

'Oh, you don't?' he asked sarcastically. 'And what do you suggest I do? Prepare a little banner saying "Congratulations" and hang it up outside for when they decide to return? What's his telephone number?'

Katherine gave it to him, knowing that she had no choice because he would simply force it out of her, and, as she expected, there was no reply.

He slammed down the receiver and scowled.

'Well,' she said, 'they're not going to run to the first place they know you'd check, are they?'

'Which is why you're here. You know his haunts. Where would he be likely to go? They're probably planning to get married in some obscure place in the morning.'

Katherine took a deep breath. 'Let them.'

'I will not let my sister's life be ruined by an opportunist.'

'David is not an opportunist! You would know that if you spoke to him for ten minutes! Why are you so suspicious?'

'Why do you think?'

'All right,' she said with a weary sigh, 'I understand that you're protective of your sister, that you don't want her to be taken advantage of, but don't you see there's nothing you can do?'

He thrust his hands into his pockets and began pacing

through the room, his face harsh. He didn't like what she was saying. Perhaps he had thought that she would be as eager as he was to stop it. After all, as far as he was concerned, she and David were lovers.

'I just don't want her to be hurt,' he said heavily, stopping to look at her. 'She may have been brought up with a great deal of money, but it has never spoiled her. If this man is exploiting her, then I don't know how she'll cope with it.'

'He's not exploiting her,' Katherine repeated in a tired voice. 'You seem to believe that the whole world is out to get their hands on money, at whatever cost, but you're wrong. True, there are a lot of opportunists out there, but there are also a lot of good people, people with principles. David and your sister are in love, and to be honest, seeing you now, I can understand why they did what they did.'

'And what is that supposed to mean?'

'Well, look at you!' she threw at him. 'Storming through the house, racking your brain for a way to lay your hands on them before mean, exploitative, callous David, who's probably concealing a history of crime as far as you're concerned, does the unthinkable and drags your sister kicking and screaming up the aisle just so that he can get his greedy hands on her money. They're in love, and the spectre of you doing your utmost to break it to pieces was too much for them to bear.'

'I'm not that bloody unfair,' Dominic said, but there was a certain amount of discomfort in his voice. 'And why, might I ask, are you defending this, when your lover has walked out on you?'

'Because David is not my lover, and he has never been my lover.' She looked at him steadily.

'You lied, in other words.'

'You jumped to the wrong conclusions and I didn't try

and correct you. Firstly because it was none of your business anyway, and secondly because he asked me to pretend that we were closer than we were, so that he and Jack could see each other in relative peace and privacy.'

Dominic moved towards her. 'You mean you knew all about this?' His voice was as sharp as a knife but she refused to be browbeaten into cowering submission.

'I knew nothing of any of this,' she said calmly. 'But if I had known how violently you would react to their relationship, then I certainly wouldn't have tried to stand in their way. People,' she said bitterly, 'deserve to try for some happiness, don't they?'

There was a thick silence between them, then he sat down next to her, his weight depressing the cushions on the sofa.

'It's a damn cowardly thing, eloping,' he said, but his voice wasn't as suffused with anger as it had been.

'Perhaps they thought that it was the only way their love would survive you.'

'I'm not an ogre,' he said, sliding his eyes across to her face.

'You could have fooled me.'

'Do I frighten you? Would you have done what they did?'

'I don't know,' Katherine said, realising for the first time how quiet the room was, how dark and still. 'You would have had to have given her her freedom at some point,' she said, to break the silence. 'You would never have been able to run her life for her, choose her husband, and even if you had, there's no telling that your choice would have been the right one.'

'So, in other words, you're saying that I should accept this.'

'With grace.'

He raised his eyebrows as though that was stretching it a bit, but he didn't say anything.

'Now,' she said, standing up, 'perhaps you wouldn't mind dropping me back to my house, now that my usefulness is at an end? Or else I could get a taxi.' She looked at her watch and saw that it was after one. Heaven only knew how easy it would be to find a taxi at this time in the morning.

'I can't drop you back,' Dominic pointed out mildly. 'Claire is asleep upstairs. Spend what remains of the night in one of the guest bedrooms. I'll lend you a shirt to sleep in.'

It was a sensible suggestion, and still she felt as alarmed by it as if he had asked her to strip and do a dance on the low marble table in the middle of the sitting-room.

'It's a lot of trouble,' she said, while the muscles in her face seized up in frozen horror. 'The beds are probably all unmade. It really would be easier if you called a taxi.'

'There are eight bedrooms,' Dominic drawled, 'and the beds are all made.'

'Oh.' She tried a thankful smile. 'In that case, of course.' What else, she asked herself, could she say?

She stood up and followed him to one of the guest bedrooms on the third floor, then he vanished and reappeared a few minutes later with a towel and a shirt.

'Claire is being collected by a school-friend's mother. I don't suppose you want to avail yourself of the lift, so I'll drop you when I go in to work in the morning.'

'That's very kind,' Katherine replied faintly, clutching the towel and shirt tightly. She waited until he disappeared back down to the second floor, then she changed quickly and quietly into his white shirt, rolling up the sleeves. It dwarfed her. It reached down nearly to her knees, and when she looked at herself in the mirror she saw that she resembled a thin little waif.

She had worn his shirts before. When they had been lovers and she had walked around his London flat, fixing their breakfast, smiling when he had reached out for her and drawn her close to him.

She blinked away the image of the past and lay down, thinking that she would never be able to sleep, knowing that he was one floor down, but sleep she did, soundly and comfortably.

When she next opened her eyes there was a bleak, grey light trying its best to fill the room, and Dominic was sitting on the side of her bed, watching her.

'I brought you some tea,' he said, and she sat up hurriedly, feeling exposed.

'What time is it?'

'A little after nine.'

'Oh, no,' she groaned.

'I looked in on you about an hour and a half ago but you were so fast asleep that I didn't have the heart to get you up.'

The curtains were still drawn tightly, and she wished that they weren't, because they filtered out the light and gave the room an unreal, unsettling shadowy feel.

'You'll be late for work,' she said illogically.

He didn't answer that. Instead he said, 'I apologise about last night. I never even thought that amid all that was happening you might have been terribly upset at David's actions. You may not have been lovers, but your hope for a relationship with him must have died with that note on your doorstep.'

His words were so unexpected that for some reason she felt herself on the verge of tears.

My hopes for happiness, she could have told him, died the day you threw that ring into the pond in Regent's Park.

She found it difficult to speak, and she looked down at her hands, entwined on the quilt.

'You look like a child in that,' he said softly, and when she raised her eyes to his she felt suddenly disorientated. There was something there on his face, an expression which she couldn't quite define, an intent which she struggled to understand.

She stared, mesmerised, waiting for him, waiting for the kiss which she knew would happen.

CHAPTER EIGHT

HIS mouth touched hers with gentle, persuasive force. He didn't push her back against the pillows but pulled her towards him, cradling her head with his hands, while he explored her soft lips with his tongue, groaning as the kiss deepened and she reached out to entwine her fingers behind his dark head, bent towards her own.

The dividing line between right and wrong, between sense and madness, seemed to have blurred. She knew that this deep, desperate yearning could be satisfied, but that satisfaction would demand its price. She drew back and he looked at her and said seriously, 'I still want you. It's not something I've wanted to admit to myself, and it defies all the laws of common sense, but I still want you.'

She noticed that the word love did not appear, but that she did not expect. He didn't love her. When he sat down and thought about it, he probably didn't even like her very much. The past was too strongly remembered for that. But he wanted her.

'If you want me to stop, then say so. I will.' His face was inches away from her own and she looked at its dark, angular lines with a mixture of desire and sadness.

How true it was when they said that a taste of honey was worse than none at all. She felt suddenly robbed by him of her future, as the knowledge came that when he walked out of her life he would take with him everything she could possibly hope to give another human being.

'I don't know what I want,' Katherine whispered honestly. 'How can you make love to someone you dislike?'

'I don't dislike you,' he said huskily. 'I did once and for a very long time but, seeing you again, I've learnt to put you and everything we went through into perspective. It would have been convenient, admittedly, if the attraction had died along with everything else, but it hasn't.'

He said that so matter-of-factly that she closed her eyes to block out the pain.

'You know what I'm offering you.'

'Tell me.'

'All right, then. What I'm offering you is a relationship with no strings attached and no questions asked. No going over of old ground.'

'A relationship with no past?'

'If you want to put it like that.'

And no future, she thought. But what have I got now? she asked herself. And what have I had for the past six years?

She pulled his head towards her and they sank back against the pillows and this time his deepening kiss was more urgent, more hungry, and she could feel his body pulsating with the same passion which was going through her own.

She moaned as his mouth moved to caress the slender curve of her neck, arching her back, her eyes closed.

Was this retribution, she wondered, for what she had done once in innocence? Never knowing that her actions would have such disastrous consequences?

He was unbuttoning the shirt, pulling it open to expose her naked breasts, and he raised himself slightly, so that he could look down at her.

He stood up by the bed and she watched in fascination as he stripped off his shirt, then the remainder of his clothes. She watched the powerful width of his shoulders, the firm, muscular torso tapering down to his hard, aroused manhood.

With an easy, graceful movement, she sat up towards the edge of the bed and her mouth instinctively found that throbbing, erect focus of his passion.

She had been living in a darkened room, she thought, just simply getting through the days, but now the room was flooded with light and she had an overwhelming feeling of coming back to life.

She was breathing quickly as her hands slid gently along his waist, trailing against his thighs, while she continued to rouse his desire with the steady, rhythmic movements of her mouth.

When she lay back on the bed again, her body eagerly yielded to his, and she cried out as he brushed his lips against her breasts before his mouth fastened to her nipple, drawing on it with a deep hunger that made her shiver with response.

With his fingers, he traced the swell of her other nipple, caressing it, playing with it, feeling the hard nub with the soft pad of his thumb.

Since Dominic, she had been untouched, her body stored away in a kind of deep freeze, and now she felt it burst into flame.

She let her legs drop open and took a deep, shuddering breath as he feathered a wet trail with his tongue along the flat planes of her stomach, down to where the source of her need ached for fulfilment.

His tongue drove into the heart of her, and he only looked up once to say hoarsely, 'Wait for me.'

Then again he began his hungry torment of her body. She writhed against his exploring mouth, and when she felt that she could no longer stand the unbearable pain of wanting, he straightened up and thrust into her, his movements deep and long and filling her with an excitement that made her want to scream out.

Her fingers curled into his back, tightening as his hand covered her breast and massaged it, and finally slackened when the crescendo of their lovemaking reached its blinding finish.

They were both still breathing heavily, though, as they lay on the bed alongside one another.

It should, she knew, have been an awkward moment, but it felt so entirely right to be lying on the bed next to him that she gave a small sigh of contentment and turned to face him.

'Another childhood fallacy blown to the winds,' he said with a crooked smile.

'What fallacy is that?'

'The one that schoolteachers never make love.'

Katherine laughed softly. 'Their babies are all delivered courtesy of the stork?'

'Somehow that never entered the childhood equation.'

He pulled her towards him and she covered his leg with her own, feeling the warmth of his body and needing it as she needed the air she breathed. It seemed almost as essential.

So what happens next? she wanted to ask. Where do we go from here? But she knew the answers to those questions. He wanted involvement on the physical level, and if she started asking for more, if she even hinted at it, then he would retreat.

And anyway, asking questions would do her no good either. She was being given the opportunity of having a part of him, of having a part of what she so deeply needed. To express anything but an adult, nonchalant acceptance of that would have been to expose herself more than she wanted.

At the end of it all—and end it would—she would at least be able to shake hands with a smile on her face. Wasn't that the way these sophisticated games of seduction were played? Rules to be followed, laws laid down, manoeuvres strictly within the lines.

'I have to get in to school,' she said. 'If we leave now I can be there by lunchtime, once I've changed into something more suitable.'

'Were there any men?'

'The nativity play is tomorrow. Today is general pandemonium day. One day before the nativity play and only two days before the school breaks up.'

'Tell me.'

She looked at the cleanly chiselled profile and said, 'No.'

Dominic shifted so that he was looking at her, giving her the benefit of those penetrating green eyes.

'How come?'

Katherine felt her face suffuse with colour. 'Well,' she said, trying to make light of it, 'I'm not the most alluring siren in the world, and besides, it's not easy to find a playmate when all your friends are happily married.'

'You looked damned sexy last night,' he said huskily.

'I don't normally wear camisoles instead of shirts,' she replied, thinking in a confused way that, although that was true, she certainly hadn't felt uncomfortable. When she was with him, it somehow felt right to do all the things and wear all the things which she normally wouldn't. That puzzled her. It seemed to ask a question, but when she tried to find the answer it slithered away, just out of reach.

'Wasn't David in favour of being a playmate?' His voice was as light as hers, but there was a brooding intensity in his eyes that made her feel stupidly happy. She slapped down the happy feeling. There were limits to how many delusions she could live under, and delusion number one was that he could be in any way jealous of a past liaison.

'Never seriously. I think we both knew the limits of what we had and we both knew that we would jeopardise a good friendship if we put the limits to the test.'

'I suppose the fact that he's got some sense, somewhere, might mean that this business with my sister isn't quite as horrendous as I first thought.'

He absentmindedly reached out to caress her breast and she said, feeling her body stir once more into life, 'I wish you wouldn't do that when we're trying to have a conversation.'

'Do you?' he asked, but there was wicked delight on his face and she gave him a dry, lazy smile.

'I have to admit that it's a bit out of character for David to run off with a woman. I always thought that he would be more likely to fight the battle by drawing up a list of reasons why, but that's a good sign, isn't it? It means that he must be head over heels in love with Jack.'

'You have a persuasive way with words.' His hand moved lower, parting her legs, cupping the moistness in between her thighs, and she sighed unsteadily, which made him laugh, a low, sexy laugh.

'Keep talking,' he said, bending and licking her nipple with his tongue, and sending darts of exquisite pleasure racing through her.

She tried to ignore the attention being paid to the various parts of her body.

'I would,' she said, eminently satisfied as his dark head moved against her breast and his mouth nuzzled against her, 'if I could remember what I was saying.'

And then it became impossible to ignore what he was doing to her. Every touch seemed to herald some new sensation and this time their bodies met in an unhurried unison, though just as sweet.

It was nearly one before she insisted that it was time for her to leave. Really and truly.

'I can't be here when Claire returns,' she told him, standing up and heading for the shower.

She let herself into the cubicle and he did as well, closing the door behind them.

'Saves on water,' he told her, which made her burst out laughing.

'Is that why you've done it?' she asked.

'No.' And he then proceeded to show her exactly why he had decided to share the shower with her, so that it was nearly two before she was finally dressed, back into last night's outfit which was ridiculously unsuitable for daytime wear.

'What are the ethics behind sleeping with the parent of one of your pupils?' he asked in the car on the way to her house, and Katherine frowned.

There *were* no ethical guidelines to this, or at least none that had ever been made clear to her, but then again, it was hardly a situation which arose on a weekly basis.

'I would rather that Claire didn't know anything about it,' she said eventually, and he nodded.

Why, she asked herself, turning to stare out of the window and not seeing much of what she was staring at, does that make me feel so awful?

She knew why, of course. In fact, she hardly had to think too hard about it.

What Dominic had offered her was a physical relationship that would exist in a vacuum, and Claire would be a complication, an unnecessary one as far as he was concerned. He wouldn't want her to start thinking that there was anything more to what they had, would he?

Whatever he said, or failed to say, on the subject, she knew that deep down he must wonder whether she would start pursuing him for something which he had no intention of offering.

'Will you be coming to the nativity play tomorrow morning?' she asked him, as the car pulled up outside her house and he switched off the engine and turned to her.

'I would not miss it for the world.'

'Santa will be visiting them on Wednesday,' she said brightly.

'So I have been informed. I have had to dampen down thoughts of the reindeer putting in a similar appearance.'

So easy, she thought, to love again, when the spectre of the past was locked away. But for how long? And did it matter? She was not strong enough to fight her love for him. She would take what he offered because martyred self-righteousness was not a warm companion on a cold winter's night.

'Spend Christmas Day with us, Katherine,' he said, just as she was about to let herself out of the car, and she turned back to him with an expression of surprise.

'But we agreed that Claire would know nothing about...us.'

'I shall tell her that you had nothing planned, so I invited you across to be kind. A French couple will be there as well. Very distant relations. They're in London for Christmas, and they're going to come up and spend Christmas Day here. They have two children, so Claire will hardly notice that you're there after a while.'

'Please don't feel sorry for me,' she said in a low voice. 'If you have plans, I would hate to intrude on them.'

'I'm not asking you because I feel sorry for you.' He looked away with a dark flush, and she wondered whether this meant that she had hit the nail on the head first time.

She had always been proud, had always thought hard before accepting favours, but pride appeared to be hibernating, and the only thing she could think of was how wonderful it would be to spend Christmas Day with the man she adored, even if her adoration would have to be under wraps.

And anyway, what good would it do her staying in her house, roasting a little chicken because a turkey was too large? Being at the receiving end of phone calls from friends, whose invitations she had already turned down, and who would want to make sure that she was all right? She loved them dearly for their concern, but it would hardly make for a festive atmosphere.

'I should love to come,' she said quietly, 'but only if you let me prepare the meal.'

'I've already booked a restaurant to take care of that,' Dominic said, resting his head against the window-pane and looking at her. 'They'll deliver it all in the morning and have assured me that even a fool would be able to follow their instructions on doing what little cooking's needed.'

'Cancel them.'

'No.' He smiled that easy smile that made her heart flutter. 'But come early, anyway. At nine. Claire would appreciate an audience for the great ceremony of opening the presents.'

She watched as his car swung up the lane and away from the house, and her heart was singing.

She was being utterly insane, playing with fire as though she hadn't already been burnt, and still she felt more lightheaded than she had done for a very long time.

I've probably made the biggest mistake in my life, she told her reflection in the mirror later that night, or at least the second biggest mistake, and I'm about to compound it by continuing to see Dominic Duvall. I am a complete idiot.

*　　*　　*

She conducted the nativity play from the sidelines the following day with a suitable expression of efficiency, and didn't once look into the audience to try and catch his eye, even though she knew exactly where he was sitting because she had glimpsed him entering earlier on.

He left when all the other parents remained to have coffee and discuss the formidable talents of their offspring. Katherine smiled and nodded and didn't take a great deal in.

Only Santa the next day, with his guffaws and his bag of presents and the chaos he engendered in his wake, brought her back down to earth, and that was simply because she found that she just didn't have the time to think of anything else apart from keeping her class in touch with planet earth.

She had arranged to go to a party on Christmas Eve—a group of mostly teachers and their other halves. It was something of a tradition, the equivalent, she supposed, of the office party, but without any of the raunchy scenes behind the photocopier which she had always vaguely assumed permeated the average office party.

It was only on Christmas morning, when she woke at six, that she delivered to herself the stern lecture which she knew was unavoidable.

This is nothing, she told herself. Your head needs to be firmly screwed on if you're going to survive with him. You will not look at him meaningfully, or make any approach, or even hint that you might want to touch him. You will certainly not let him see that you're not the cool adult he assumes you are, ready to have a fling simply for the sake of physical attraction.

She arrived at the house at precisely nine o'clock, to find Claire in a state of near-uncontrollable excitement, and

Dominic standing in the background with an indulgent, amused smile on his lips.

'Santa came!' Claire told her repeatedly, as they went into the living-room. 'I have hundreds of presents!'

Katherine caught Dominic's eye over his daughter's head, and they smiled, a smile of such intimate conspiracy that she immediately looked away.

Claire was jumping round the tree, poking the presents, rattling them, hardly able to contain herself, and Katherine grinned. It was the first Christmas she had spent in the company of a child. She had forgotten quite how exciting the whole thing was in the eyes of a five-year-old.

They sat by the tree, with Claire between them, and watched as presents were opened, marvelled at, turned round and round, while Claire innocently exclaimed at how wonderful Santa was to have bought her everything on her list, and really she must have been a very good girl indeed to have deserved that.

'Leading up to a request for chocolate,' Dominic said drily to Katherine. 'And of course she knows,' he continued over Claire's head, 'that the ploy won't work, because there will be no chocolate until after lunch.'

'But I got a bunny box from Amy,' Claire pointed out, 'and since it's mine...' Her eyes were pleading and Katherine smiled. The logic of children could be irrefutable sometimes.

'I don't think Santa would approve of chocolates at this hour in the morning,' Dominic said, for want of a more handy excuse, 'and I would agree with him.'

The chocolates were promptly forgotten, and when she was ensconced in the heap of toys surrounding her, he turned to Katherine and said in a low voice, 'I got you something.'

Katherine went red. 'I didn't get you anything,' she stammered.

'I think I'll overcome the blow of that,' he said, with a slow smile which almost made her forget several of her resolutions. He handed her a parcel, a book, and she opened it and saw that it was a slim paperback called *How To Overcome Your Mother's Influence*, which made her burst out laughing.

'Are you trying to tell me that I should be on a psychiatrist's couch?' she asked, grinning and looking down at the volume.

'Oh, I think the couch bit could be reserved for me,' he drawled, and she awkwardly tried to rise to the occasion with something witty, which fizzled out into fairly inaudible mumbles.

'But,' he said, not looking at her but idly looking at Claire, who was busy dressing and re-dressing her new dolls in various sets of clothing, 'you do need to let go of those bits of your past that are still hanging over you. Your mother may have had her opinions of you, and doubtless made her thoughts perfectly clear, but it's time you shrugged that off and realised that you're your own person now.'

'Oh.' Katherine looked at him from under her lashes. 'You feel sorry for me. I'm really quite an independent woman, you know.'

Dominic's eyes shifted over to her and he shook his head with an expression of resigned impatience, but whether he intended prolonging the conversation or not, Katherine didn't know, because Claire was now fed up with playing on her own.

She enlisted their input and, until the caterers arrived at eleven, they found themselves trying to figure out how to erect the doll's house, which proved to need the genius of a mathematician and the skill of a cabinet-maker.

'It's wonderful!' Claire informed them, awestruck, once the thing had been fitted together.

'It looks precarious,' Katherine commented, tilting her head at an angle to scrutinise it.

'Aren't these things made of wood any longer?' Dominic complained lazily. 'When I was a boy, there was none of this plastic stuff around.'

'But that was a hundred years ago,' Claire said gravely, and Katherine smothered a laugh.

She couldn't remember having had such a good time on Christmas Day. Ever.

Last year, she had opened her small collection of presents with David, and they had had a quiet day at his mother's house. And the same the year before that, and the year before that. And when she dredged up memories of her own childhood Christmases, all she could remember was sitting cross-legged under the tree, opening her small parcels one by one under the eagle eye of her mother, who would make scathing remarks about most of them. She couldn't remember anything like this atmosphere of joyous glee and anticipation.

The caterers arrived, laden with food, and shortly afterwards Dominic's guests arrived, a couple in their mid-thirties, with their two young children, and Claire vanished, seemingly for the remainder of the day, reappearing for lunch and making nearly as much fuss over the nonsense in the crackers as she had done over the much larger gifts she had opened earlier.

It was only later, when the guests had gone, leaving behind them the usual chaos that seemed to accompany children wherever they went, that Katherine wondered where David and Jack were and what they were doing.

Presumably they were now entrenched in a state of married bliss. They, at any rate, had overcome their hurdles. How ironic that their victory had left her own life in a state of flux, because she doubted that she and Dominic would ever have made love had it not been for them. The situation would simply never have arisen.

She curled her legs under her and sipped her coffee, liking the warm glow that filled the room from the fire burning in the grate, liking the feeling of peace she had at being here, in this house, with Dominic upstairs settling Claire. A very domestic scene, she thought. A very domestic day, in fact. She knew that if she wasn't careful she would end up being lulled into a dangerous illusion that this might just last forever.

She didn't look up when he entered the room, and he said, with a smile in his voice, 'You look like a cat sitting there in front of the fire.'

'I'm hypnotised by the fire,' she said, glancing at him as he settled on to the sofa next to her. 'In a minute I'll start braving myself to face the cold outside.'

'Why?' he murmured, reaching forward to take his coffee-cup from the table in front of them, and then looking at her over the rim of the cup. The green eyes were fathomless in the darkened room. As mesmerising as the fire and a lot more lethal.

'It's called going home,' Katherine told him, 'at the end of a very enjoyable day. Thank you.'

'You don't want to go,' he said, depositing his cup on the table and then doing the same with hers. 'You don't want to uncurl your body from this chair, you don't want to get into your coat, you don't want to drive back in the dark to an empty house.'

When he spoke like that, in that deep, velvety voice that

seemed to hold the answer to every question she could ever ask, she could feel the blood stir thickly in her veins.

'No, I don't,' she agreed, 'but that doesn't mean that I'm not going to.'

He stretched towards her and curled his fingers in her hair and pulled her towards him, so that she was lying against his body and could hear his heart beating through his shirt.

He slowly unbuttoned her blouse. She could feel the brush of his fingers against her skin and her body quivered.

'You want to stay here with me,' he murmured into her hair, and he slipped his hand under the blouse and cupped her breast. His fingers played with her nipple, stroked her stomach, edged beneath the waistband of her skirt.

He held her captive, and the thought flashed through her mind that perhaps this was precisely what he wanted. To gain entry into her life so that he became the one calling the shots, so that he could be the one who dictated the length and breadth of their relationship.

'No,' Katherine said softly, 'you want me to, and I'd really like to know why.'

'Because,' he said, breathing deeply against her neck, 'I'm a fool.'

Or, at least, that was what she thought he said, and she squirmed to face him. Tomorrow, she thought, tomorrow she would sort everything out in her mind. Tomorrow she would put an end to this lovemaking which would kill her in the end.

She knelt on the sofa and opened the blouse, guiding his head to the valley between her breasts, and as he kissed them she flung her head back, offering herself to his mouth, a willing victim.

With unsteady fingers, she unclasped the waistband and the skirt fell around her thighs.

Dominic groaned, a low, hoarse sound, and pushed her back against the sofa, quickly pulling down the skirt, and through the lacy underwear he massaged the aching mound of her femininity. She shuddered and moved against him, and he slipped his hand beneath the lace and she stifled a deep groan of satisfaction.

How could she think when her body was in flames? She had been asleep before he arrived, before he crash-landed back into her life, and his first kiss had awakened her from her slumber. She felt alive now, in tune with everything around her, and not like someone trapped in some strange limbo of vague contentment, unable to move forward.

She saw that his hands were unsteady as he removed his clothes and that gave her a heady sense of power.

She had never understood, then, why he had found her attractive, and she could understand it even less now, but she refused to stop and analyse the questions that that raised. She stretched out her arms and, as it covered hers, felt the weight of his body with a great surge of love and desire. She wrapped her arms around him and felt the tight muscles beneath her palms with delight.

He had both breasts in his hands and was giving them his undivided attention and her body relaxed so completely that it was as if all her bones had melted under the heat of their lovemaking.

He pulled her up towards him so that they were facing each other, and with an easy movement she eased herself on to him, feeling his hardness move inside her, feeling at one with him in a way she knew that she could never feel with anyone else.

She watched his face as they reached the pinnacle of pleasure, and as he exhaled a long breath of satisfaction she impulsively kissed him on his neck, a small, chaste kiss that contained everything she had ever felt for him and everything she ever would.

He opened his eyes and looked at her.

'I know we said that we would never discuss this,' he murmured, 'but there never was a man, was there? You didn't walk out on me for someone else.'

'No.' She looked back at him and trailed her finger along his cheek, then along the strong, determined line of his jaw. 'No, there was never another man.'

'Why didn't you say so from the beginning?'

'I had my reasons,' she said, looking away with a frown.

It wasn't true that they could dissect their lives like a piece of meat, cutting away the past, snipping the edges of all the uncomfortable bits. She had known that all along, but she had preferred to let herself be persuaded by him that it would work, that they could make love and ignore everything else that threatened to intrude on that.

'It doesn't matter,' he said, curling a strand of hair around his finger and staring at it absent-mindedly.

It does matter, she thought, disturbed. It may not to you, because there's no emotional involvement on your part, but it matters to me.

'I need a shower,' she said, standing up and haphazardly putting on her clothes.

'Not yet.' He pulled her down again so that she was sitting on the edge of the sofa.

Katherine looked at him. In the semi-darkened room, lit only by the glowing flames of the fire, there was something almost unreal about him. His long, powerful body was so perfect, so exquisitely fashioned, that he seemed to have stepped out of a myth, a Greek god reclining in lazy abandon next to her.

No god, though, she thought, just human. A human being with all the usual human failings. What would he say if she were to entrust her story to him? Would he still give her that devilish, charming smile? Would he be able to dismiss the past so easily?

She stood up and began walking towards the top floor, sprinting up the stairs to the shower.

She was hardly surprised when he joined her, but her thoughts, this time, were somewhere else. And she could see that he was tuned in to the fact that her mind was a million miles away because he didn't try to touch her. He simply watched her, his face inscrutable.

'You look as though you need a drink,' he said, once they were dressed, and she glanced across at him with a worried expression.

'Why do you say that?'

'Because,' he muttered, 'contrary to popular belief that I'm utterly and completely insensitive to other people's feelings, I would have to be blind not to see that something's bothering you.'

She followed him down to the drawing-room and accepted a glass of brandy, a drink which she secretly abhorred, but they did say that it gave you courage and, right now, she felt that she needed all the courage she could lay her hands on, because the time had come. There was no point in pretending that this temporary vacuum they had created for themselves could exist indefinitely. It couldn't.

No, she thought, taking a long swallow of the liquid and feeling a hot sensation rush down her throat, the time had finally come for the truth to be told.

'Dominic,' she said, putting the glass down carefully on the table next to her, 'there's something I feel you ought to know.'

CHAPTER NINE

DOMINIC didn't say anything. He just sat there on the chair, cradling his glass in his hands, but Katherine could feel the shift in the atmosphere. There was a sudden watchfulness about him that made the hairs on the back of her neck stand on end. Even the room seemed to have become colder, although the fire was still burning as brightly as it had been half an hour ago.

Now that she had come to this, of course she didn't know where to start, but he was clearly in no rush for her to start anywhere, because he didn't say a word. In a way, his silence was even more alarming than if he had bombarded her with a series of questions.

She looked at him from under her lashes, and took a deep breath.

'It does matter, you know,' she said, realising that she was starting at the end, or at least somewhere in the middle, and not at the beginning as she had intended. 'I know you say that we can just sweep the past under the carpet, as though it's some kind of inconvenient bug that can be hidden away and forgotten about, but it's not going to work for me.' She twined her fingers together, then untwined them, a nervous movement that helped to distract her from the sickening rush of nerves she felt in the pit of her stomach. 'It would be so easy if we could just bottle up the unpleasant things in life, the things we don't want to remember, and pretend that they never really existed, but I can't do that.'

'There's no need to drag it all up now,' he said, and his voice startled her. 'Do you think that a confession will cleanse your soul?'

'Something like that, I suppose.'

'You told me yourself that there was no man. Were you lying?'

Katherine shook her head desperately. 'No, I wasn't lying.'

'I didn't think so. It seemed all wrong at the time. It didn't make sense.' He had been leaning forward with his elbows resting on his knees. Now he relaxed back and looked at her from under his lashes. 'You were afraid,' he said calmly. 'Everything happened quickly between us and somewhere along the line you panicked and took flight. It happened. It's over and done with. We've both learnt lessons from that.'

'You don't understand!' The words were wrenched out of her, and she anxiously began pacing the room, trailing her fingers along the edge of the sofa, over the gleaming bits of furniture, along the glass-fronted cabinet along the wall of the room.

'Start at the beginning.' His voice was calm and she realised that he thought he knew it all, but he was wrong, and she couldn't think where she ought to begin. Wherever she started, it would be the wrong place, but there was no backing out now. Things had to be said which, she knew, should have been said a long time ago.

'Yes.' She stopped behind the sofa and rested against the back of it and looked at him.

The beginning. The moment her father had walked through the door and never come back. Wasn't that where it started? The years she had spent as a child, then as a teenager, growing up to believe that, whatever she possessed, it was never quite as much as everyone else did.

'My mother,' she said slowly, 'was a difficult woman. I don't mean to sound self-pitying, but I never really had a great deal of self-confidence. I suppose over the years it all drained away from me and later, when I could understand why she had been the way she had, I just didn't know where to start to put it back together again.' She looked at him to see whether she could spot any incipient signs of boredom, but there were none. He was listening intently, his head crooked to one side.

'I never had much excitement,' she continued, without bitterness, 'and I really don't think I ever missed it. At least, not so much that it ever occurred to me to rebel. Of course, I had my daydreams, but mostly I was content to study, because studying was the only way I could see of ever escaping. I wanted to be a teacher, you see. Do you think that was a very dreary ambition?'

'A very brave one,' he said in a low, sympathetic voice. The sympathy was what made her wince. She didn't want sympathy.

With a sudden flash of insight, she realised what he thought. He thought, in retrospect, that she had walked out on him because she hadn't had the self-confidence to believe that she could ever marry and keep a man like him. He would have thought that without any vanity or arrogance, simply as a statement of truth. That was why he had given her that odd Christmas present. If only it was as simple as that.

'When my mother died,' she said, with a sigh, and with a feeling that this was uphill going all the way and no hope of it getting any easier, 'I moved up here and took a job at the school I'm teaching at now.'

'Did you think that everything would change?' he asked gently.

'It was the first taste of independence I'd ever had,' Katherine admitted. 'It was not as sweet as I had hoped, but I was happy anyway.'

'Until one day you decided to go to London and see for yourself what else there was out there. Katherine, I understand, believe me.'

'You only understand a small part of it,' she said in a voice stronger than she felt inside. It was as though he had gathered together the pieces of a jigsaw puzzle and slotted them all together, but the picture he had was a one-dimensional one. It seemed to make sense; it was only when you looked at it from different angles that you could see the inaccuracies, the gaps, the missing links.

'I had been teaching for a while, and everything was moving merrily along, when I began to get headaches— dreadful, blinding headaches.'

He hadn't expected that. He sat up and looked at her and the alertness was back on his face once again.

'I could hardly concentrate on what I was doing,' she said. She could remember as though it was yesterday the agony of lying in bed with the lights dimmed and a cold compress over her eyes. Every movement had hurt. It had even hurt to think. 'In the end, I decided to go to the doctor and he sent me along to the hospital to have a scan done. I can't remember what the technical word for it was, but he said that it would show if there was anything seriously wrong. He seemed to think that it was stress. He said that people underplayed the importance of stress and only realised it was there when something like that began happening.'

He had been very sympathetic. He hadn't acted as though she was a deranged woman fabricating symptoms which didn't exist. She still went to the same surgery now, although that particular doctor had long retired, replaced by a doctor who seemed only just to have outgrown his boyhood acne. Katherine always thought with amusement that that was a sure sign that she was getting old.

Dominic stood up and poured himself another drink, and he remained standing, as though there was a sudden restlessness in him that couldn't be contained.

'And then what?' he asked tightly. He raked his fingers through his hair and drank a bit more from the glass.

'I went along. They did whatever they had to do and said that the results would be with the doctor within a week, but in fact my doctor telephoned me before that. He said that he needed to see me immediately.' She put her hand to her forehead and realised that it was shaking, either from the sheer power of her memories of that time, or else from the near-panic she felt at the thought of continuing.

There was no longer any sympathy on Dominic's face. His expression was shuttered and somehow alarming.

'Go on,' he grated.

'Of course, I knew that something was wrong. Doctors never get in touch with you unless the news is bad, do they? Usually, you assume that if you don't hear from them, everything's all right. Anyway, I went along suspecting the worst, but nothing I suspected could have been as awful as what he had to say. I don't want to go into the details of that conversation, I still feel giddy when I think about it now, but the upshot was that I was given months to live.'

There, it was out, and she couldn't bring herself to look at him. She knew, without having to see, that what little he had felt for her had turned to ice.

'That was when I decided to go to London. I wanted to throw away all my inhibitions and live a life I had never tasted, even if it was going to be for a short while, so I got in touch with my friend, and that's where it all began.'

She looked up at him and her fingers clenched on the back of the sofa as she saw the shock on his face give way to the icy depths of dislike.

How, she wanted to scream wildly, could she have known that she would meet *him*? By the time she had become involved, her deception had been so embedded that there was no way that she could tell him the truth.

He didn't say anything, not a word. He didn't have to. His eyes said it all on his behalf.

'I hadn't given anyone my forwarding address,' she continued, compelled now to finish what she had begun. 'I explained to the principal that I needed compassionate leave of absence, but I didn't tell her where I was going, so I never received the letter from the surgery. It was waiting for me after—when I returned here. In the meantime, the headaches had gone. I didn't think about that. I assumed that that was just the natural course whatever I had would take. Please say something, Dominic,' she pleaded.

'What is there for me to say?' he asked coldly. 'I certainly can't tell you that I understand, because I don't.'

'I never suspected that you would come along!' she cried out.

She stretched out her hand to him and he looked at the gesture with a distaste that seemed to have frozen him into immobility.

'You might as well finish,' he said in a grim voice, and she nodded miserably.

'I gather that they tried desperately to get in touch with me. My doctor went and saw the principal and explained the situation and they tried various ways to find me, but in the end they had to give up. I had vanished, and every avenue they took led to a dead end. You see, it had been a bureaucratic mistake. The results of the tests that they'd given my doctor referred to someone else who happened to have the same surname.' A tear spilled down her cheek and she wiped it away with the back of her hand.

'And why,' he asked, in the same flat, glacial voice, 'didn't you tell me about your condition at the time? Why?'

'I just couldn't. I never thought…never imagined…' She had spoken so softly that she didn't know whether he had heard, but she wasn't going to repeat herself, and she wasn't going to launch into a retrospective explanation because she could see from his face that anything she said would simply bounce off him now. He would have been prepared to forgive her insecurities, but he would never forgive her deception.

She could see clearly enough how she must appear to him. A selfish monster who had used him in the worst way possible, conducting an affair with him when she had known that it was leading nowhere.

How could she explain that she had simply been carried away on the wings of something so wonderful that by the time she had realised how deeply she was involved, it had been just too late?

He had told her how much he admired her openness and she had been open, yes, in everything but that. She had not been able to bring herself to tell him that she was living with a time-bomb ticking inside her, waiting to detonate. She had known that she had fallen so sweetly headlong into love, and it was only later, when it had dawned on her that the impossible had somehow happened, that he was as involved with her as she was with him, that she had realised that she had to end the relationship.

What, she wanted to ask, would he have done if she had told him the truth? How could she have done that to him? He would either have walked away or else he would have felt compelled to stay with her to the end, and how could she have put him through that? I was weak, she wanted to say, but in the end, I left the way I did because of *you*, because I loved you. And then, later, when she had found out that it had all been a mistake, a terrible mistake, she had already realised what her subconscious had been telling her all along, that their worlds were too different, that she had pretended to be someone she wasn't, and that in reality they were little more than two individuals, hurtling through space, briefly making contact and thinking that the contact bound them, when in fact it had only emphasised, quite clearly to her, how dissimilar their orbits were.

He had fallen in love with a mirage. He hadn't fallen in love with a teacher with a dowdy wardrobe of clothes, he had fallen in love with a bright young thing dressed in borrowed finery. How could she hope to recreate the magic? The mistake that had set her free had in the end nailed her firmly to reality.

'No,' he said with biting sarcasm, 'you just couldn't say anything, could you? It was just much easier to ride the roller-coaster you had found. What a shock it must have been when I proposed to you. Was that when your scruples got the better of you?'

'No, you must see that—'

'I see what's staring me in the face!' he roared. 'It was all one complicated web of deceit from beginning to end! And to think that I thought you were the one in a million, the one woman who was as transparently clear as running water. It would have been better if there had been someone else,' he snarled. 'At least then you could have been excused on the grounds of passion. As it is, what you've just told me shows you for what you are—a cold, scheming bitch, who didn't think twice about using a man for what he could provide. You wanted excitement and you took it without a backward glance, knowing that the limits to what you could give in return were as rigid as the cords of a noose around your neck!'

'Don't say that!'

'Why?' he sneered. 'Does the truth hurt?'

'I admit that what I did was wrong... I was weak, yes, but I was never manipulative.'

'I'm surprised that you bothered to tell this sordid little tale,' he said, ignoring her. 'I'm surprised that you didn't just take what was on offer once more.'

She didn't say anything. What was there left to say? She felt numb, like a block of ice, drained of everything.

I loved you then, she wanted to say, and I love you now. But she couldn't bear the thought of the mockery those admissions would evoke.

She walked across to her coat, slipped it on, and said in a low voice, 'I think you will agree that it's time for me to leave.'

Was it only a few hours ago that she had been enjoying the best Christmas she could remember? Was it only a few hours ago that she had been eating a meal and laughing around a noisy table with crackers? It seemed like decades ago.

If she looked in a mirror, she was convinced that she would see a head full of grey hair. She felt a thousand years older than she had that morning.

'Was it your ambition to lose your virginity?' he asked, moving across to her with the stealth and speed of a leopard. 'Was that on your list of things to do when you started going out with me?'

'Never!'

'And did you really enjoy the lovemaking, or was that a farce as well?' he asked, overriding her protest, and she looked up at him, her eyes wide.

'What do you think?' she whispered bitterly.

'I think that that was probably the only real thing you ever showed me,' he said, staring at her as if she was a stranger he had never seen before, an enemy he had suddenly discovered in his midst. 'Well, why don't you take the memory of this with you?' And he inclined his head towards hers, and his mouth crushed hers with a force that propelled her backwards against the wall.

She struggled against him, but her efforts were useless. He pulled her head back, coiling his fingers in her hair, and kissed her with anger and hatred.

He pushed aside her coat and his hand gripped the swell of her breast and she struggled against him.

'Please!' she said, turning her head from side to side.

'But you enjoy me making love to you,' he said, his mouth against hers. 'Wouldn't you like one final act of passion?'

'This isn't passion, it's hatred!'

'It's what you deserve.' But he stood back from her, and even his posture was unforgiving.

'I was a fool,' Katherine whispered, 'but I wasn't ruthless.'

'That's debatable.' They stared at each other, then he turned away and said, with icy control in his voice, 'I shall be removing Claire from the school immediately. She won't return after the Christmas vacation.'

'There's no need,' Katherine said in a high voice. 'Don't embroil her in this. She loves going to school there! She has friends. This has nothing to do with her!'

He turned round to look at her and she could see that she was talking to a brick wall.

'Close the door behind you.' Then he moved to the bar, and the last thing she saw of him was his downbent head as he poured himself another drink. Then she flew out of the room, out of the house and away back to her own house, coldly awaiting her.

Her mind refused to think. At least not coherently. She drove far too fast through the narrow lanes, her face aching from the effort not to burst out crying.

But once she was inside the house she sat down on the sofa, without bothering to remove her coat and without bothering to switch on the overhead light, and let the tears fall down her face like a river, inadequately mopping them up with her hands because she had no handkerchief.

This will all pass in time, she told herself later, in bed. Her eyes were red and puffy and she felt exhausted from weeping. There couldn't possibly be any tears left inside her. She remembered reading a story once of a child who cried so often, and over such trivia, that one day her tears all dried up and she found that she could never cry again, even when something terrible happened. Katherine felt as though she had cried everything there was in her.

She spent the next few days in a state of dreamlike misery. She couldn't seem to rouse herself to do anything at all. Normality was just too much at the moment, a little beyond her.

She had fully expected to spend the remainder of the Christmas vacation in a state of complete isolation, but on New Year's Day the doorbell went and David stood there beaming at her, a face from what seemed a million light-years away.

'You look terrible,' he told her, 'and by the way, a very happy New Year to you.'

'I have flu,' she lied, 'and a very happy New Year to you as well.'

She tried to summon up some semblance of enthusiasm, but she wished that he hadn't come.

Jack, it seemed, was with Dominic and things, it appeared, were wonderful. Married life, he assured her, was the answer to all of life's questions.

'And have *you* seen Dominic?' she asked, with her back to him, hungry for each morsel of information about him, and angry with herself for feeling that way.

'Oh, yes,' David said. 'I thought, to be honest, that he would be far more alarming than he actually was. Poor Jack was in a state of nerves for hours beforehand, but it was all a bit of an anticlimax. He didn't seem all that bothered about the fact that we'd got married. No sermons on my unsuitability. He barely flickered an eyelash about it all. Unpredictable, I suppose, but I was well relieved, I can tell you.'

But how was he looking? she wanted to ask. Did he mention me?

'What will you do about school?' she asked, sitting down at the kitchen table opposite him and cradling a mug of coffee in her hands.

Everything, it appeared, had been thought out and worked out to the last detail, and she spent half an hour listening to David's plans for moving to the South of France, where Jack could get a job and he could find work teaching English in one of the schools, and during the long holidays he would begin writing a novel. He would write about political intrigue in a school. He was full of ideas. She looked at his face, brimming over with enthusiasm, and wished that some of it could rub off on her.

'And what about you?' he asked as a postscript, and more or less on the way out, and she shrugged her shoulders.

'What about me? School begins in a few days' time. I shall carry on there as normal. Of course I shall miss you, but I'm really so pleased that everything's worked out between you and Jack. I'm sure you'll be very happy.' There didn't seem a great deal left to say on the subject.

'I'll miss you too,' David said, standing by the door and throwing her a rueful smile. 'But of course, I shall keep in touch, and whenever we're up this way we'll make this our first point of stop-over. After Mother, of course.' He laughed, and she laughed with him because they both knew how possessive his mother was about him.

The house seemed empty after he had gone, but his visit did do one thing: it made her snap out of the torpor that had filled her for the past few days. She spent the day vigorously cleaning the house. She filled five dustbin bags of rubbish. She went through her wardrobe like a tornado, parcelling up clothes which she would never wear again.

Six years ago she had left Dominic Duvall, because she had wanted to spare him the unutterable pain of watching her decline, because she had wanted to spare him more hurt. And then, too, she had been so convinced that he had only seen in her those things which she did not really possess. And maybe, to a large extent, she had been right. Maybe if he had met her without the sparkle and the glitter that initial attraction would not have been there.

But she was never going to take refuge behind drab colours again.

She went into Birmingham for the January sales, and spent money without thinking too hard about it. She bought bright things, colourful clothes, some new ornaments for her house. She would wallpaper the sitting-room. She had been meaning to do it for years but had never got round to it. At the back of her mind, she thought that now she would have all the time in the world to get round to all those things which she had not done before.

It gave her a great sense of purpose, and she actually

managed to go a long way to convincing herself that life could carry on without Dominic Duvall.

She would miss Claire, though. She had become accustomed to that serious little face in her class; she had enjoyed watching her progress from timid bystander to a child who had gradually begun to join in.

She was stunned, when she went in to school on the first day back, to find that Claire was there, in her uniform, waiting with the rest of the class for lessons to start.

She waited until three, after school had finished, then she called Claire up to her desk and said gently, 'It's wonderful to see you here. Your father mentioned that he might be sending you to a different school.'

Claire gave her a proud little smile. 'I said no.'

'You said no?'

'I told him that I did not want to go to another school, that I like this one, that I liked *you.*' The smile wavered a bit. 'You do not mind that I used your name?'

'I'm glad you're back.' She squeezed the small hand resting on the top of the desk, and grinned. She could imagine how furious he would have been, being held to ransom by a child.

'Jack is going to France at the end of the week,' Claire said, apropos of nothing in particular. 'She said that I can go and stay with her any time I want. She said the weather will be better than over here. The house you and Daddy built for me has broken.'

'I'm sure he'll mend it.' She had to look away, because the memory of that fleeting bond of intimacy between them didn't bear thinking about.

'Will you tell him to?' Claire asked quickly, with a frown.

'I think you should.'

'He's never around,' Claire argued. 'He is going out with a lady-friend.'

Katherine's face froze and she cleared her throat. 'Perhaps his lady-friend could give you a hand,' she said. Things move on, she thought with pain. People get married and move away, life carries on. Did you expect him to pine? He might have been physically involved with you, but he wasn't emotionally involved. There must have been dozens of lady-friends waiting round the corner, ready to snap up a catch like Dominic Duvall. That's life, isn't it?

'I hate her,' Claire said bluntly, still frowning. 'She fusses in the kitchen and she won't let me eat fish fingers for tea.'

'That's no reason to dislike her,' Katherine said, trying without much success to sound bright and cheerful when all she could think was that someone else was touching his body, seeing him smile, hearing his deep, velvety voice and probably feeling the same way that she had.

'She wears too much make-up,' Claire carried on, caught up on her own momentum now. 'She's no fun. Not like you. Can't you come and cook for Daddy?'

'I'm a very poor cook,' Katherine said briskly. 'Now, love, it's time you hurried back home. You're doing very well with your reading. You mustn't forget your homework. Three pages tonight.'

Talking was difficult. Her throat felt as though it was closing over and, even though she was saying the right things, her mind had veered off on a completely different tangent, and it was making her feel slightly sick and giddy.

'But will you come and visit?' Claire pleaded, and Katherine nodded vaguely. 'When?'

'Soon,' she promised.

'Today?'

'No, love. I'm busy today, but another day.'

'But you have to come today,' Claire protested. 'Gail is coming over to cook and I don't want to eat her food!' Tears of frustration were welling up and Katherine said, in the same brisk voice, something about home cooking being much healthier than fish fingers and that carrots would make her hair grow.

She stood up and walked Claire out to the entrance, feeling that she had to get some fresh air.

The little voice was still grumbling at her side and she walked out of the building quickly, towards her car, and rolled the window down because she felt hot, even though it was freezing outside and dark, with a heavy fog which had been there all day.

The cold wind on her face would help her to think. She needed to think, to get her thoughts in order. She drove out of the car park with her mind in a whirl, down the lane with her thoughts crashing about in her head, making her feel hot and feverish. She told herself that she was over-reacting, that if this was how she was going to behave whenever some passing mention of his name was made in her presence, then she was in for a rough ride for the rest of her life.

The last thing she remembered thinking before she lost control of her car was that she was a sensible woman, a grown woman, and that she had to stop acting like an adolescent suffering from unrequited love.

The tears made her vision blurry and she felt the impact before she lost consciousness and slumped across the steering-wheel.

When she came to, she was in a room, on a very hard bed with a very stiff pillow, and facing a television set which was perched in the air and supported by a high-tech contraption which enabled it to swivel around, presumably at the discretion of the viewer. Katherine looked at the television set and let herself slowly remember what she was doing in a hospital. Then she buzzed a little red light next to the bed and waited for someone to come.

She ached all over, in places which she had never even known existed. Every bone in her body seemed to be independently hurting and, as soon as the nurse entered, she said faintly, 'Hello. Might I have some painkillers please?'

'Ah.' The nurse consulted a chart clipped to the bottom of the bed, smiled brightly and said no. 'Not until you've seen the doctor, dear.'

'Please,' Katherine said, wishing that she could fight off this feeling to cry which overcame her on a regular basis. 'I want to go home.'

'I'm afraid not.' The nurse looked sympathetic but firm, and Katherine thought that she would probably make a very good schoolteacher. 'I'll just fetch Dr Sawyers, dear.' She bustled out and returned within five minutes with a doctor who smiled, sat on the edge of her bed, and listed her injuries with mathematical precision. Two broken ribs, a broken wrist and a severely twisted ankle.

'You're lucky it wasn't more serious,' he said, smiling, as though this was a very happy moment for him indeed. He stood up and informed her casually, 'I gather your car's a write-off, though.' Which was the final straw. She burst into tears, gulped, and blew her nose vigorously with her undamaged hand into a wad of tissues which the doctor handed her.

'Shock,' he said wisely. 'I'll get Nurse to fetch you some painkillers, and I want you just to rest as much as you can.'

'How long am I going to be here?' she wailed, and he gave this some thought.

'At least a week, but then you can go if there's someone to look after you. Is there someone to look after you?'

'No,' she said, gulping, and he frowned worriedly.

'Well, don't worry about it,' he murmured in a soothing, bedside voice. 'Something can be sorted out.' And he whisked himself off and was instantly replaced by a nurse, who took her temperature while talking incessantly, felt her pulse, took her blood-pressure, and then, last but not least, handed her two painkillers.

'I expect you'd like a cup of tea,' she said, and Katherine smiled gratefully.

'And a phone, please.'

And then, after making a call to the school, she settled down to feel thoroughly sorry for herself.

She had asked two of the teachers at the school to bring her in some reading matter when they came, because she strongly felt that her brain would turn to pulp if she watched television constantly for a one-week period, and was cheered considerably when they arrived with arms full, lots of school gossip, and several drawings which her class had done.

Katherine held the drawings this way and that and decided that she wasn't nearly as badly off as the pictures they had done depicting her.

'I'm covered in plasters and blue in this one,' she laughed, holding up one of the drawings, but she propped them up next to her after her friends had left, and smiled every time they caught her eye.

She had asked for a couple of books, great big ones, but over the next two days, as the pain subsided a little, she found her thoughts drifting off in the direction of Dominic, wondering about this woman in his life, wondering whether it was serious, and forced to conclude that their brief contact had had very little impact on him if he had found it so easy to jettison her and find a replacement.

It's much better this way, she told herself without conviction. It's easier to forget a man if you know, for sure, that he's relegated you to a mental rubbish-heap somewhere at the back of his mind. But she didn't feel much better for thinking that.

And, also, she had begun to think about what she was going to do once she had left the hospital. Both her friends had assured her that they would be around, making sure that everything was all right, and she would be able to hobble about, but how was she going to cope with the loneliness, cooped up in her tiny house, without twenty schoolchildren to take her mind off things?

She placed the book on her stomach and stared out of the window. Her job was out there, her house, her garden, and a huge vacuum where her life should have been.

She heard the door open and she turned round, glad for whatever company had arrived, even if it was just the chattering nurse clutching a thermometer, and then all her pain went away in a rush of adrenaline as her eyes focused on Dominic, standing by the single white snap-together wardrobe. Tall, dark, powerful Dominic, the last person she wanted to see because he was the only one she so desperately needed to.

CHAPTER TEN

'OH,' SHE said tonelessly, while her mind struggled to come to terms with the man standing in front of her. 'What are you doing here?'

'What happened?' He glanced around for somewhere to sit and finally dragged the chair by the window next to her bed.

What do you care what happened? she wanted to ask. The last time I laid eyes on you, you couldn't wait to get me out of your house. The last time I heard your name mentioned was in connection with another woman.

'I crashed my car,' Katherine said bluntly, fingering the tail-end of her plait and sliding her eyes around him so that she didn't actually have to look him in the face. 'The weather was very bad and I took a corner a bit too quickly. And, now that the pleasantries are over, would you mind telling me what you're doing here? How did you even know that I was in hospital?'

'Claire told me,' he said heavily, sitting back and stretching his legs in front of him so that his feet were almost touching the little white cabinet next to her bed. 'She asked me to help her with a card she wanted to make for you.' He fished inside his jacket pocket and extracted a folded piece of paper, on the outside of which was a sweetly irrelevant picture of a house and a garden, and inside a little get-well message in large, childish writing, which sloped up the paper and virtually disappeared off the edge. Katherine smiled, but the smile disappeared as quickly as it had come.

'There was no need to hand-deliver it,' she said stiffly, sticking it up alongside the others she had received.

Thank heavens for friends, coming to visit, rallying round. It was all she had, she realised, as a single woman.

'No,' he agreed into the stilted silence, 'there was no need.' He sighed and ran his fingers through his hair, an oddly impatient gesture which she watched with a cool, detached expression.

'Then why are you here?'

'What do you intend to do when you come out?' he asked, skirting over her question in a way which frustrated and angered her.

'I really don't think that that's any of your business,' she said, maintaining her composure with a perverse sense of triumph. A bit of a shame it had so thoroughly deserted her in the past. She could have done with some of this cool composure when she had been struggling to fight off the dangerous attraction she had felt for him.

He didn't say anything to that, although he looked uncomfortable.

'Tell Claire thank you very much for the card.'

'The doctor said that you have no one to look after you when you come out.'

Katherine went bright red and clenched her fists into tight balls. 'What right have you got to question my doctor about something like that?' she said through gritted teeth.

'He thought that I might be able to help.'

'Yes, yes, you could help. You could help a great deal by leaving this room. We've said enough to each other.'

'No, we haven't,' Dominic said, folding his arms and looking at her. 'We haven't begun to say anything to each other.' He gave her a long, cool stare, as if he was throwing down a gauntlet and had already steeled himself for the inevitable fight.

'Oh, get out,' she muttered wearily. 'I'm too tired to cope with this.' She raised one shaking hand to her forehead and rested against it.

'Katherine,' he said, and that challenging note was still in his voice, 'I've come to take you home.'

'I'll get a taxi,' she informed him, not looking at him, staring down at the white coverlet. However did they get their sheets to be quite so hard? she wondered. Were they designed to be as uncomfortable as decently possible, so that patients wouldn't be tempted to malinger on much-needed beds?

He stood up, walked round the bed to the wardrobe and opened the door. Then he started packing her clothes into her bag, cramming them in, and she looked at him with open-mouthed horror.

'What the hell do you think you're doing?' she asked in a high voice. She would have jumped out of the bed, but her injuries put paid to any such spontaneity. 'I'm not due to leave for another night!' she said, in as loud a voice as she could manage without bringing a stream of nurses in to see what was going on.

'The doctor said that you can leave now, provided you have someone around to take care of you on a constant basis.'

'Will you get your hands off my clothes?'

'No.' He continued packing, and when he was finished he turned to her and said in a very calm voice, 'I was told that you were lucky to have escaped so lightly. If the impact had been only a little harder, you might not be here today.'

'And what a great loss to the world that would be.'

He moved swiftly across to her and held her wrist in his

fingers, and when he spoke there was a furious edge to his voice.

'You stupid, selfish, stubborn, thoroughly infuriating creature, Katherine Lewis,' he grated. 'I should just walk away from here. I should just leave you to wallow in your own self-pity.'

'Why don't you?' She glared at him, and there was a long silence.

Then he said roughly, turning away, 'Because I damn well can't.' A red flush had appeared on his neck and his voice was savage.

'And what is that supposed to mean?' She knew what she would *like* it to mean, but she was finished living in dreamland. Reality was getting on with things, not pretending that there was anything left between them, any little morsel of love from six years back.

'Oh, shut up,' he said, which made her even angrier.

'Don't you *dare* tell me to shut up!' she snapped.

'Why? What are you going to do? Leap out of bed and punch me? You can't do any leaping, woman, with broken ribs and a twisted ankle.'

'The ankle is much better,' Katherine snarled. 'And you might as well put that bag down because I have absolutely no intention of leaving here with you.'

He ignored her. He walked across to the door, vanished, then reappeared a few minutes later with the doctor, a feat which bordered on the miraculous because, she thought acidly, doctors were never around when you wanted them. They flitted in and out of their wards at a marathon pace, generally leaving a trail of unanswered questions behind them, because it was difficult to get your thoughts in order when you had to fire questions like a bullet from a gun to a consultant who appeared to be on the run.

'Ah, Miss Lewis,' the doctor said brightly. 'Mr Duvall here says that he'll be taking you home.'

'Oh, he does, does he?'

'There's no reason for you to stay here. You're well bandaged up and you appear to be healing well. Your own local doctor can have a look at the bandages every couple of days. I'll be in touch with him. I can prescribe some strong painkillers for you, if you feel that you need them, but really, I find that most patients do much better if they recuperate in their own homes.' He smiled a smile of camaraderie at Dominic, which got on her nerves. 'No domestic chores for a while, though,' he said, and Dominic laughed, his green eyes roving over her.

'We'll work round that one, Doctor.'

'Excellent, excellent.'

Katherine opened her mouth to protest but, before her vocal chords could oblige, Dr Sawyers had gone, and she looked at Dominic with dislike.

'Now look at what you've done. There's no convenient twenty-four-hour-a-day companion at my house to take care of me.'

'You don't think that I intend to deposit you on your doorstep with a broken wrist and cracked ribs, do you? You must still be in shock after the accident, if you think that.'

He stepped aside to let the nurse in, complete with wheelchair and the usual bright smile which appeared to be some kind of job regulation.

'I refuse to leave this room,' Katherine stated flatly, which threw the nurse into a dither of uncertainty.

She stammered hesitantly, looked to Dominic for guidance, and was clearly relieved when he said in an authoritative voice, 'Leave her to me, Nurse.'

'Leave me to you?' Katherine turned to him as soon as the nurse had left the room. '*Leave me to you*? I would rather be left to a pit of vipers. The last time I saw you, you informed me that you never wanted to lay eyes on me again. Now you turn up here and start giving orders and you expect me...you expect me to just fall in with you?' She was so angry that she had to stop speaking, because she knew that anything she said would just degenerate into a series of inarticulate splutters. And she hadn't even got round to the topic of Gail whatever-her-last-name-was as yet.

'Yes.' He didn't elaborate on that. He just scooped her off the bed, deposited her on to the wheelchair, eyed her grey cardigan and tracksuit bottoms dubiously, and asked, 'Will you be warm enough in that?'

'Dominic,' she said, 'why are you doing this?' She wished that she was more mobile, mobile enough to head off down the hospital corridor at a running pace, so fast that he would never catch up with her. 'Do you feel guilty? Because the last time you saw me we parted in anger, and now here I am, bedbound? Is that it?'

'Don't be stupid,' he muttered under his breath. He took her coat and placed it over her legs.

'Stop telling me not to be stupid!'

'Stop arguing with me. You won't win. I've come to take you home and nothing you say is going to stop me.'

She felt a curious excitement spread through her at the way he said that, in that darkly, angrily possessive voice, and she just as quickly resented her wayward emotions. For a moment, she had felt a wild surge of hope fill her, and hope was something she never wanted to feel in her life again. Hope ignored too many unavoidable questions; it ignored his real feelings towards her, the dislike, the dis-illusionment, and it ignored the woman he was now seeing, making love to and—who knew?—perhaps even falling in love with.

So she maintained a tight-lipped silence through the formalities of departure and in the car, which was chauffeur-driven and waiting outside the hospital for her, and was only swamped in confusion once again as the car drew up outside his house and she was lifted inside, even though she informed Dominic that she could walk, that she wasn't a complete invalid.

'You can be a maddening person,' he said, placing her on the sofa in the living-room and then sitting next to her, so close that her breathing became all erratic.

'I can't stay here,' she answered, lowering her eyes.

'You can't stay anywhere else,' he muttered. 'I've discovered that not having you around is bad for my health.'

Hope reared its head again and she fought it down, but it was getting harder. There was a look in his eyes that was telling her things that he wasn't saying with his mouth and that she desperately didn't want to believe.

'I've been a fool,' he said. 'I was a fool to let you walk out six years ago; I was a fool not to have raced back to try and find you.'

She didn't think that she could say anything even if she wanted to, which she didn't.

'When you turned me away, I felt as though my world had collapsed. I'd never let myself get close to anyone the way I'd let myself get close to you, and when you told me that it had all been a game, that there was someone else involved, I could have killed you. I went back to France and did the worst possible thing. I got involved with someone else, and then everything that followed was just a series of complications.' He pressed his thumbs against his eyes and sighed. 'The marriage was a farce from the word go, and at the end of it I was left with such a bitter taste in my mouth when it came to women that I never stopped to wonder how it was that for all that time I still kept on thinking about you. You just hung around like a miasma.'

'It all went wrong,' Katherine said, with a wonderful, frightening feeling of standing on the edge of a precipice. 'I'm so sorry I never told you the truth, Dominic, but it was so very hard. When I went to London, I never thought that I would become involved with anyone. You weren't a situation that I courted.'

'I know that,' he said heavily. He traced his finger along her collarbone and her skin tingled where he touched it.

'I don't think I let myself see the dangers. I was just so happy, really for the very first time in my entire life. I felt as though I had chanced upon the secret of the universe and I forgot everything for a while. I forgot about the death-sentence hanging over my head, or at any rate I shoved it to the back of my mind until I couldn't keep it there any longer, but I couldn't tell you, Dominic. I suppose partly that was for selfish reasons, but mostly it was because I wanted to spare you. Afterwards, when I returned here and read that letter and had to readjust all my perspectives, I realised that ours was a relationship that was not meant to be. I thought that you had fallen in love with someone who didn't really exist and that if you saw me, saw me for what I really was, which was a very ordinary person with very ordinary hang-ups, then you would run a mile. And I couldn't bear the thought of that, of your disillusionment.'

'Oh, Katherine.' Two words that made her heart soar.

He undid the buttons of her cardigan, then unclasped her bra at the front and drew it aside, and his finger trailed over her breast in ever-decreasing circles until he was touching the hard nub of her nipple, although his eyes were still focused on hers.

'When you told me the reasons why you had left,' he murmured in a voice that was barely audible, 'I was angry.

I had somehow convinced myself that, after you said that there had been no man involved, the reasons left, by some weird process of elimination, must be simple. I thought that you left me because you had felt at the time that you couldn't cope. Do you know, when I saw you again at that school, I managed to tell myself that I was still deeply angry with you, but the need to see you became compulsive? Just knowing that you were around, in the area, drove me mad. I couldn't get you out of my head, and then, slowly, when you began disclosing bits of your past, I thought I had it all worked out. I thought you had walked out on me all that time ago because of insecurities which went back into your childhood, and that made me feel stupidly better.'

He stopped what he was doing and looked her directly in the eyes, and then he said, 'You may know that I love you, but I can never tell you just how much.'

Katherine didn't say anything. She had fallen off the precipice but, instead of hurtling down, she was high up in the clouds, floating in a land she had only ever dreamt of.

'You love me?' she asked hesitantly, and he threw her a dry grimace.

'Always and forever. I just never stopped.' His eyes roamed over her body. 'I was stupid and blind.' He threw her a sheepish look. 'I even made the mistake of thinking that I could replace you with someone else. A most unappealing woman called Gail, who did everything she could to try and convince me that she could become indispensable if only I'd let her.'

She had been waiting for him to mention her, debating in her mind whether she should spoil the magic of the moment with questions, or whether she shouldn't simply let the matter rest and wait for it to crop up in the natural course of things.

'Gail... How did you meet her? Did you...?' She felt her heart constrict at the thought of any intimacy between him and another woman.

'I met her,' he said 'at one of those hideous parties which people feel obliged to give over Christmas. I was getting quietly drunk and thinking of you when she made her presence known in no uncertain terms. She had just returned from a two-week vacation in New York and she seemed to think that that gave her an immediate point of contact with me. And I looked at her and saw your face, and I was so angry with you, myself, the whole damn world, that I chatted to her. I heard myself asking her to dinner and I was aghast at the prospect of it, which perversely stopped me from backing down, and then, before I knew what had hit me, she was round at the house, cooking meals, trying to persuade me that being a bachelor was an unnatural state of affairs. Every time I looked at her I saw you. For a while I wanted to prove to myself that this time you had blown it, that I had learnt my lesson, that I wasn't a complete raving idiot, and the harder I tried to convince myself of that, the more I realised that I really was a complete raving idiot after all.'

'You mean...' Katherine's eyes widened in horror and she tried not to laugh.

'Oh, my darling.' His eyes were distraught. 'I was a fool, and you must believe me when I tell you that I never touched her. Not once. I wasn't even tempted. As soon as she stepped foot into the house, all I could think of was how I could get her out. She was leggy, blonde, a model— and if she had stood on the kitchen table and performed a strip-tease, I would have still found her utterly unattractive. Please believe me.'

'I do believe you,' she said, smiling, 'and besides, Claire didn't care much for her either, did she? And children are the devil when it comes to accepting strangers into their house.'

'You knew?'

'The information was volunteered by your daughter,' she said seriously, and he burst out laughing.

'I can't believe I shall have to contend with the two of you joining forces against me in the future,' he said, shaking his head. 'Because there *is* going to be a future, isn't there, Katherine?'

'There is,' she agreed lazily, covering his hand with hers. 'I love you, Dominic Duvall.'

'Yes.' He looked eminently satisfied with the response. 'I suppose all we shall have to sort out now is the where and the when.' He turned her hand over so that he was looking down at her palm, and he idly rubbed his thumb against the soft flesh, a sweet, intimate gesture that made her heart want to burst.

Had it been like this for David as well? When he realised that he had fallen in love with Jack and that his love was reciprocated? Had he had this same, overwhelming feeling of wanting to reach out and become one with her, the way she felt for Dominic? If that was the case, then it was no wonder that they had decided to sneak away and get married rather than face even the slimmest chance of having their plans dashed.

I've never known true happiness before, she thought with some wonder. Oh, I've seen a glimpse of what it could be, but when something is out of reach, it forever remains a blurry dream.

'Whenever,' she said. 'Wherever.'

'Oh, no, my girl.' He looked at her wryly. 'Now that I've finally got you, there's no way that I'm going to let you have any leeway to change your mind.' And he smiled, as if he knew very well that she would never do that, and the knowledge was inspiring. 'Besides, there's the question of Claire. A little girl with some very definite views.' He looked thoughtful. 'No, I don't think she would approve at all of my living with her beloved teacher in a state of unmarried bliss.' He grinned. 'So, whenever becomes as soon as possible, and wherever might just as well be this house. After all,' he said, 'it's going to be your home now.'

'Yes, my love.' She sighed a long sigh of contentment. 'My home.'

How long her heart had searched for that.

HARLEQUIN *Presents*

Passion™

Looking for stories that **sizzle**?

Wanting a read that has a little extra **spice**?

Harlequin Presents® is thrilled to bring you
romances that turn up the **heat!**

Every other month there'll be a
PRESENTS PASSION™
book by one of your favorite authors.

Don't miss
THE SPANISH HUSBAND
by **Michelle Reid**

On sale December, Harlequin Presents® #2145

Pick up a **PRESENTS PASSION**™—
where **seduction** is guaranteed!

Available wherever Harlequin books are sold.

HARLEQUIN®
Makes any time special ™

You're not going to believe this offer!

In October and November 2000, buy any two Harlequin or Silhouette books and save $10.00 off future purchases, or buy any three and save $20.00 off future purchases!

Just fill out this form and attach 2 proofs of purchase (cash register receipts) from October and November 2000 books and Harlequin will send you a coupon booklet worth a total savings of $10.00 off future purchases of Harlequin and Silhouette books in 2001. Send us 3 proofs of purchase and we will send you a coupon booklet worth a total savings of $20.00 off future purchases.

Saving money has never been this easy.

I accept your offer! Please send me a coupon booklet:

Name: _____

Address: _____ City: _____

State/Prov.: _____ Zip/Postal Code: _____

Optional Survey!

In a typical month, how many Harlequin or Silhouette books would you buy <u>new</u> at retail stores?

☐ Less than 1   ☐ 1   ☐ 2   ☐ 3 to 4   ☐ 5+

Which of the following statements best describes how you <u>buy</u> Harlequin or Silhouette books? Choose one answer only that <u>best</u> describes you.

☐ I am a regular buyer and reader
☐ I am a regular reader but buy only occasionally
☐ I only buy and read for specific times of the year, e.g. vacations
☐ I subscribe through Reader Service but also buy at retail stores
☐ I mainly borrow and buy only occasionally
☐ I am an occasional buyer and reader

Which of the following statements best describes how you <u>choose</u> the Harlequin and Silhouette series books you buy <u>new</u> at retail stores? By "series," we mean books within a particular line, such as *Harlequin PRESENTS* or *Silhouette SPECIAL EDITION*. Choose one answer only that <u>best</u> describes you.

☐ I only buy books from my favorite series
☐ I generally buy books from my favorite series but also buy books from other series on occasion
☐ I buy some books from my favorite series but also buy from many other series regularly
☐ I buy all types of books depending on my mood and what I find interesting and have no favorite series

---

Please send this form, along with your cash register receipts as proofs of purchase, to:
In the U.S.: Harlequin Books, P.O. Box 9057, Buffalo, NY 14269
In Canada: Harlequin Books, P.O. Box 622, Fort Erie, Ontario L2A 5X3
(Allow 4-6 weeks for delivery) Offer expires December 31, 2000.   PHQ4002

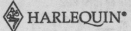